#13 ON the CASE with HOLMES and WATSON

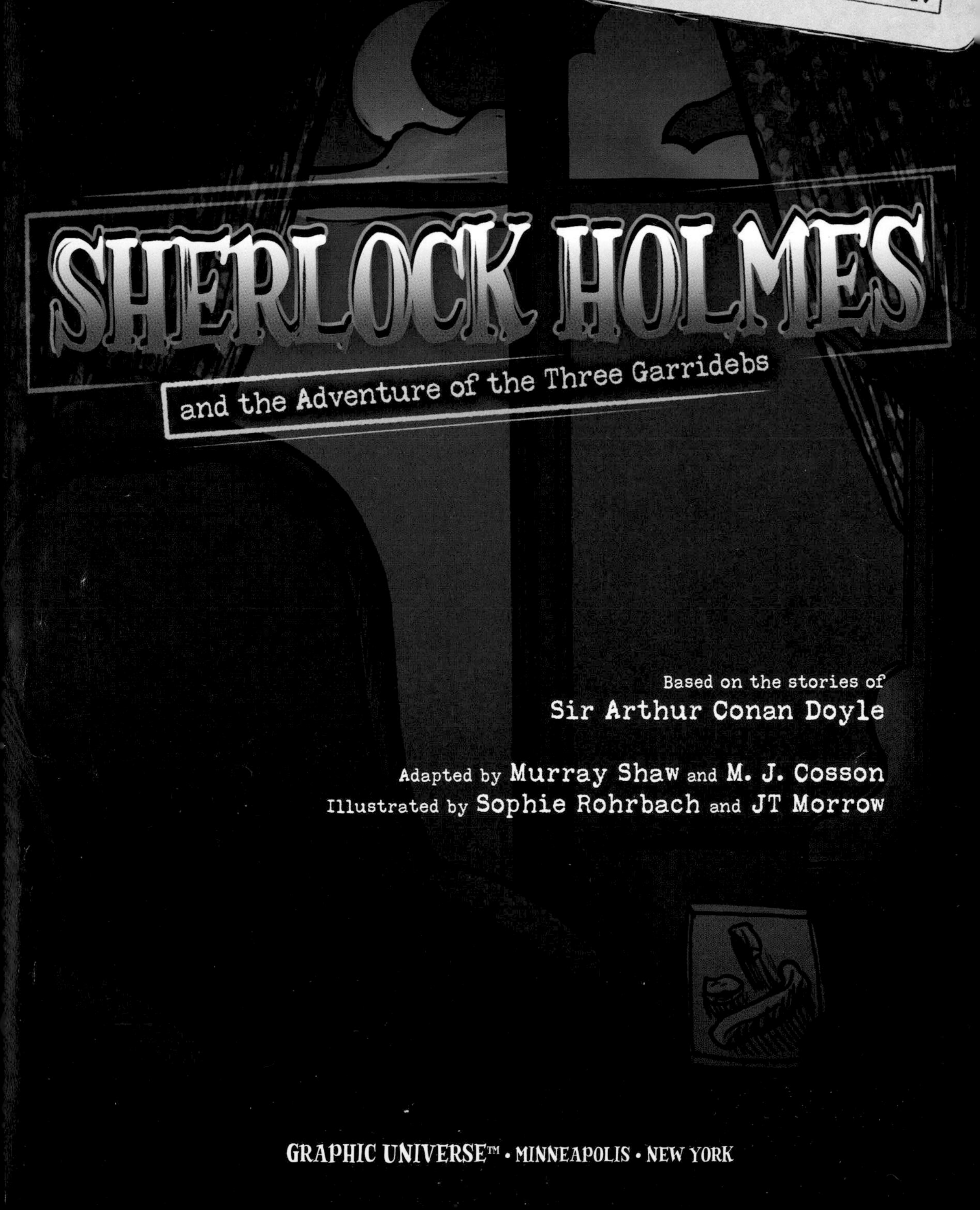

SHERLOCK HOLMES

and the Adventure of the Three Garridebs

Based on the stories of
Sir Arthur Conan Doyle

Adapted by Murray Shaw and M. J. Cosson
Illustrated by Sophie Rohrbach and JT Morrow

GRAPHIC UNIVERSE™ • MINNEAPOLIS • NEW YORK

Grateful acknowledgment to Dame Jean Conan Doyle for permission to use the
Sherlock Holmes characters created by Sir Arthur Conan Doyle

Graphic Universe™
A division of Lerner Publishing Group, Inc.
241 First Avenue North
Minneapolis, MN 55401 U.S.A.

Website address: www.lernerbooks.com

Shaw, Murray.
     Sherlock Holmes and the adventure of the three Garridebs / based on the
stories of Sir Arthur Conan Doyle ; adapted by Murray Shaw and M.J. Cosson
; illustrated by Sophie Rohrbach and J.T. Morrow.
       p   cm. — (On the case with Holmes and Watson ; #13)
     Summary: Retold in graphic novel form, Sherlock Holmes investigates
a man who claims that he will have a large inheritance if two more men
who share his surname are found. Includes a section explaining Holmes's
reasoning and the clues he used to solve the mystery.
     ISBN: 978-0-7613-7091-8 (lib. bdg. : alk. paper)
     I. Graphic novels. (I. Graphic novels. 2. Doyle, Arthur Conan, Sir,
1859-1930. Adventure of the three Garridebs—Adaptations. 3. Mystery and
detective stories.) I. Cosson, M. J. II. Rohrbach, Sophie, ill. III. Morrow,
J .T., ill. IV. Doyle, Arthur Conan, Sir, 1859-1930. Adventure of the three
Garridebs. V. Title.
PZ7.7.S46Sio 2012   2011005114
741.5'973—dc2

Manufactured in the United States of America
I—BC—12/31/11

The Story of
SHERLOCK HOLMES
the Famous Detective

Sherlock Holmes and his helpful friend Dr. John Watson are fictional characters created by British writer Sir Arthur Conan Doyle. Doyle published his first novel about the pair, *A Study in Scarlet*, in 1887, and it became very successful. Doyle went on to write fifty-six short stories, as well as three more novels about Holmes's adventures—*The Sign of Four* (1890), *The Hound of the Baskervilles* (1902), and *The Valley of Fear* (1915).

Sherlock Holmes and Dr. Watson have become some of the most famous book characters of all time. Holmes spent most of his time solving mysteries, but he also had a wide array of hobbies, such as playing the violin, boxing, and sword fighting. Watson, a retired army doctor, met Holmes through a mutual friend when Holmes was looking for a roommate. Watson lived with Holmes for several years at 221B Baker Street before marrying and moving out. However, after his marriage, Watson continued to assist Holmes with his cases.

The original versions of the Sherlock Holmes stories are still printed, and many have been made into movies and television shows. Readers continue to be impressed by Holmes's detective methods of observation and scientific reason.

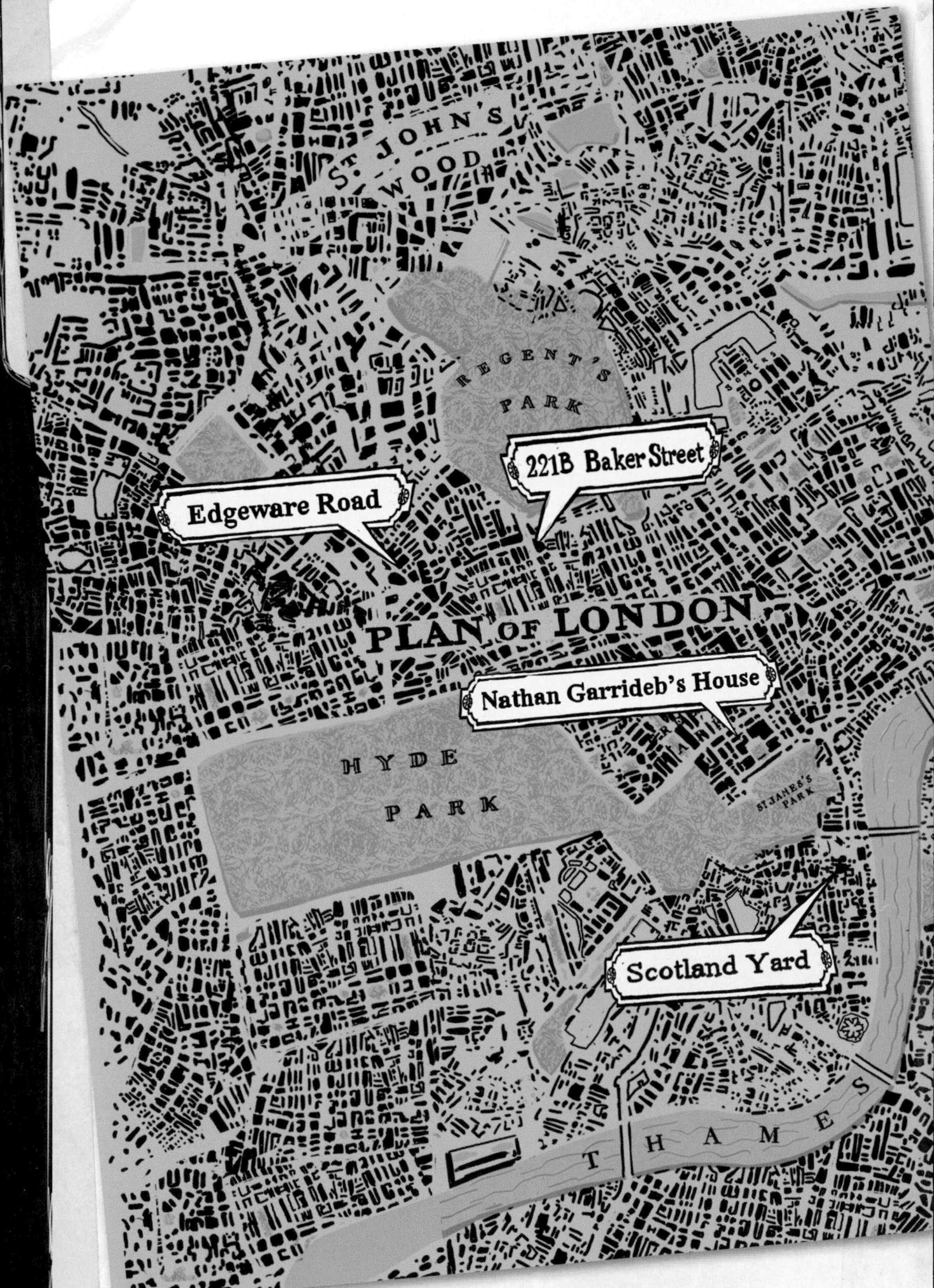
St. JOHN'S WOOD
REGENT'S PARK
221B Baker Street
Edgeware Road
PLAN OF LONDON
Nathan Garrideb's House
HYDE PARK
St JAMES'S PARK
Scotland Yard
THAMES

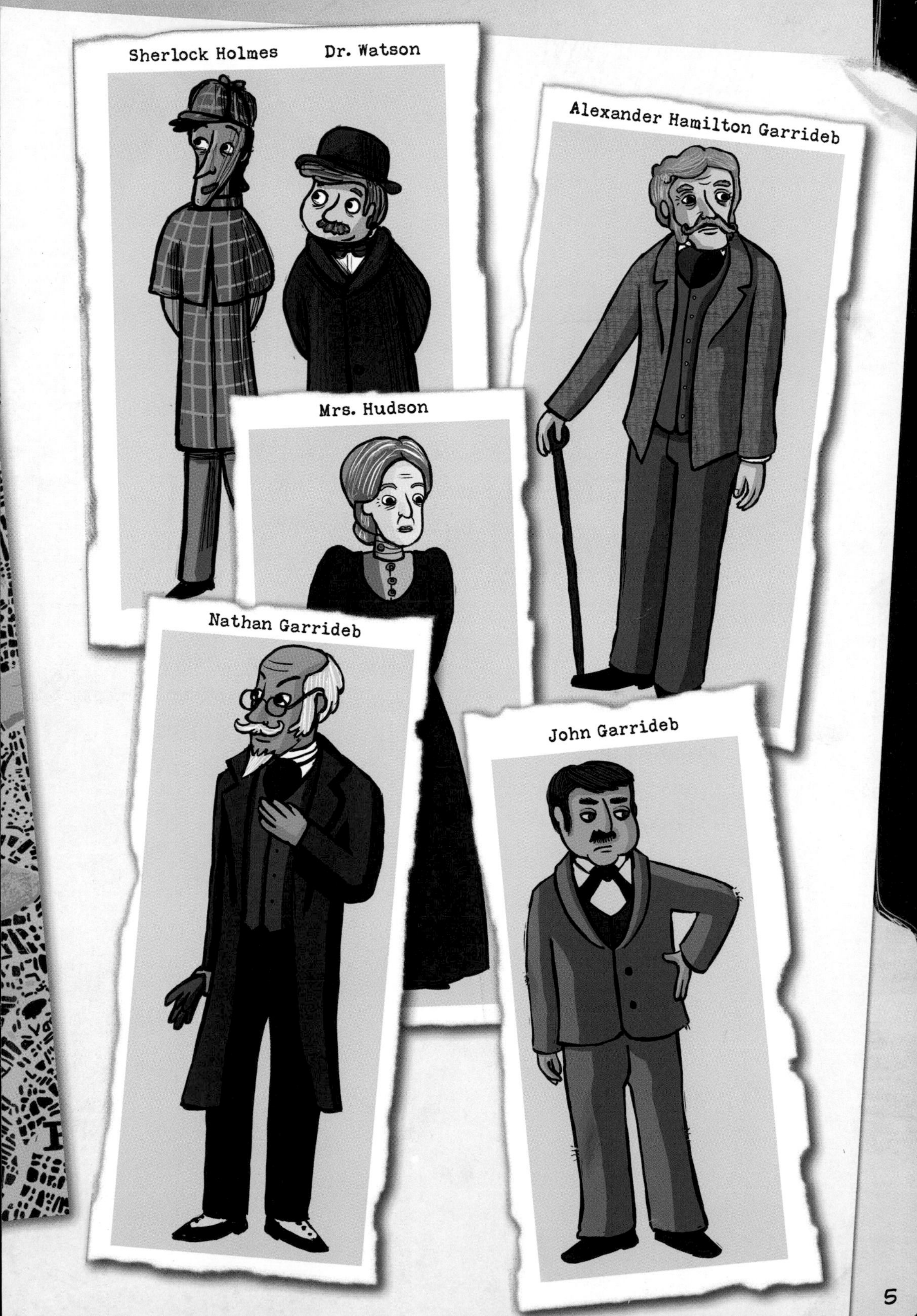
Sherlock Holmes
Dr. Watson
Alexander Hamilton Garrideb
Mrs. Hudson
Nathan Garrideb
John Garrideb

From the Desk of
John H. Watson, M.D.

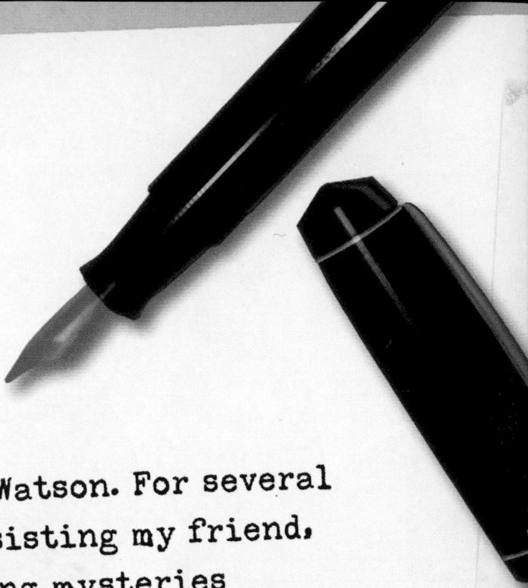

My name is Dr. John H. Watson. For several years, I have been assisting my friend, Sherlock Holmes, in solving mysteries throughout the bustling city of London and beyond. Holmes is a peculiar man—always questioning and reasoning his way through various problems. But when I first met him in 1878, I was immediately intrigued by his oddities.

Holmes has always been more daring than I, and his logical deduction never ceases to amaze me. I have begun writing down all of the adventures I have with Holmes. This is one of those stories.

Sincerely,

Dr. Watson

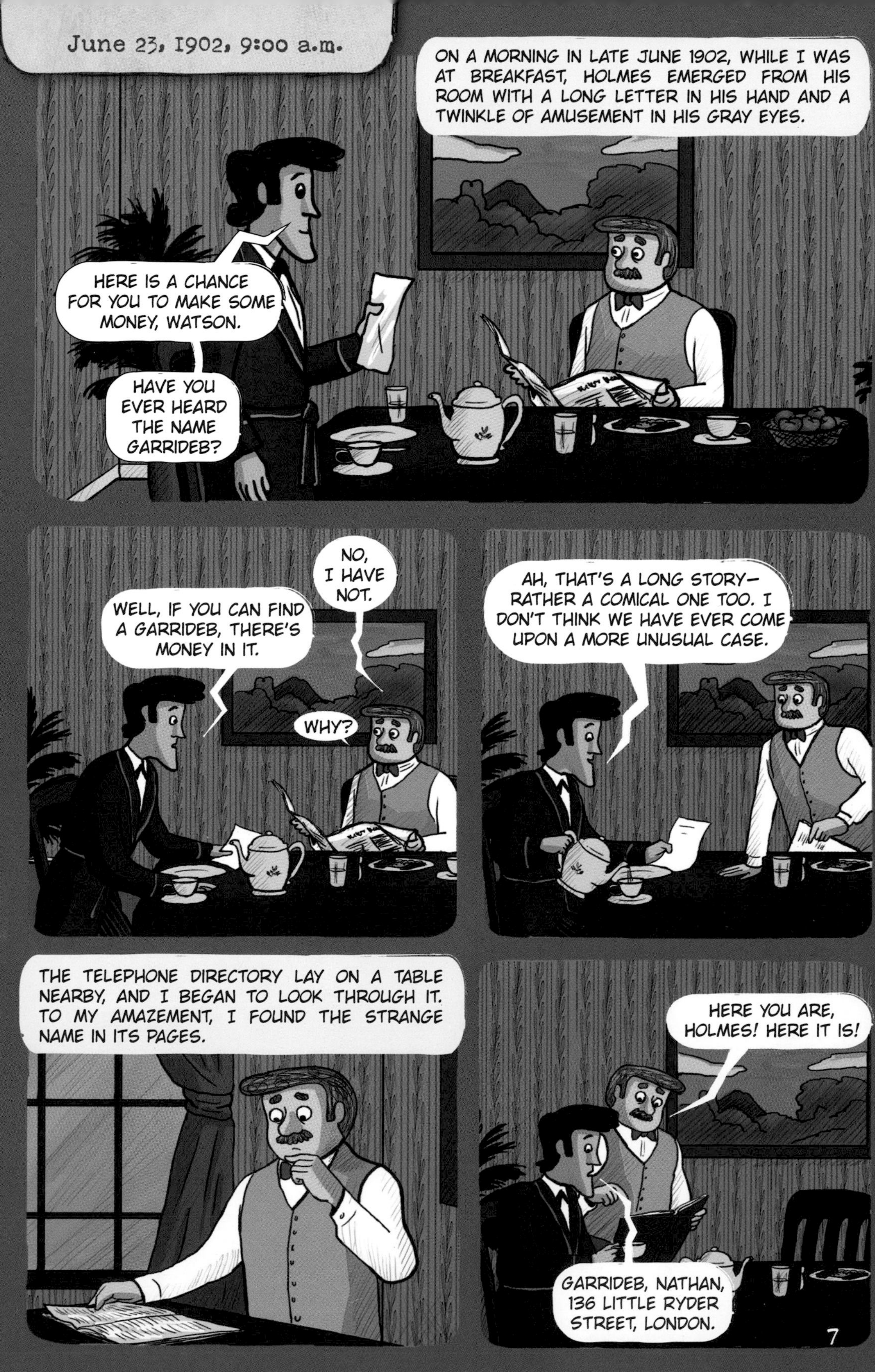
June 23, 1902, 9:00 a.m.
ON A MORNING IN LATE JUNE 1902, WHILE I WAS AT BREAKFAST, HOLMES EMERGED FROM HIS ROOM WITH A LONG LETTER IN HIS HAND AND A TWINKLE OF AMUSEMENT IN HIS GRAY EYES.
HERE IS A CHANCE FOR YOU TO MAKE SOME MONEY, WATSON.
HAVE YOU EVER HEARD THE NAME GARRIDEB?
NO, I HAVE NOT.
WHY?
WELL, IF YOU CAN FIND A GARRIDEB, THERE'S MONEY IN IT.
AH, THAT'S A LONG STORY—RATHER A COMICAL ONE TOO. I DON'T THINK WE HAVE EVER COME UPON A MORE UNUSUAL CASE.
THE TELEPHONE DIRECTORY LAY ON A TABLE NEARBY, AND I BEGAN TO LOOK THROUGH IT. TO MY AMAZEMENT, I FOUND THE STRANGE NAME IN ITS PAGES.
HERE YOU ARE, HOLMES! HERE IT IS!
GARRIDEB, NATHAN, 136 LITTLE RYDER STREET, LONDON.

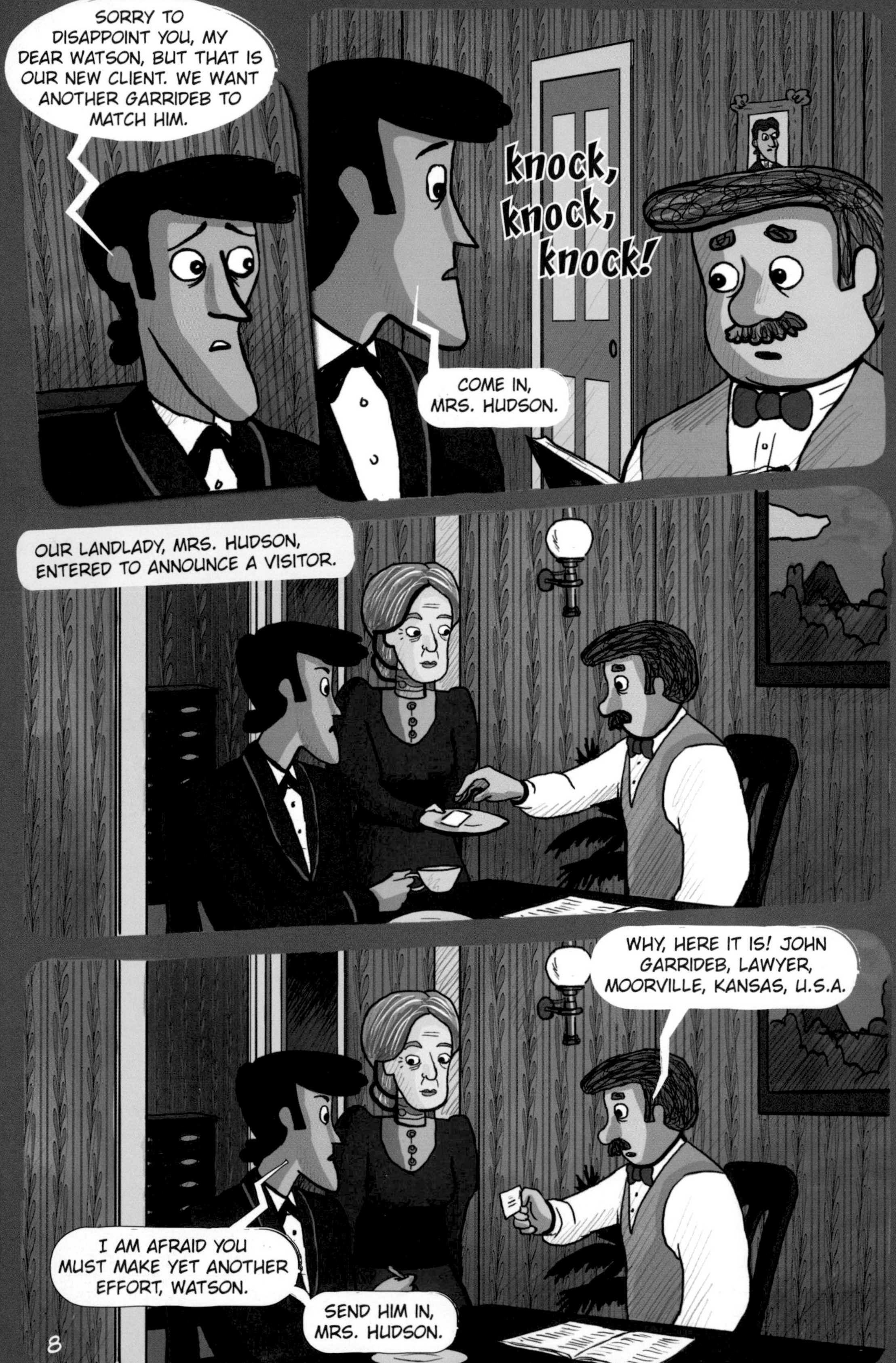
SORRY TO DISAPPOINT YOU, MY DEAR WATSON, BUT THAT IS OUR NEW CLIENT. WE WANT ANOTHER GARRIDEB TO MATCH HIM.
knock, knock, knock!
COME IN, MRS. HUDSON.
OUR LANDLADY, MRS. HUDSON, ENTERED TO ANNOUNCE A VISITOR.
WHY, HERE IT IS! JOHN GARRIDEB, LAWYER, MOORVILLE, KANSAS, U.S.A.
I AM AFRAID YOU MUST MAKE YET ANOTHER EFFORT, WATSON.
SEND HIM IN, MRS. HUDSON.

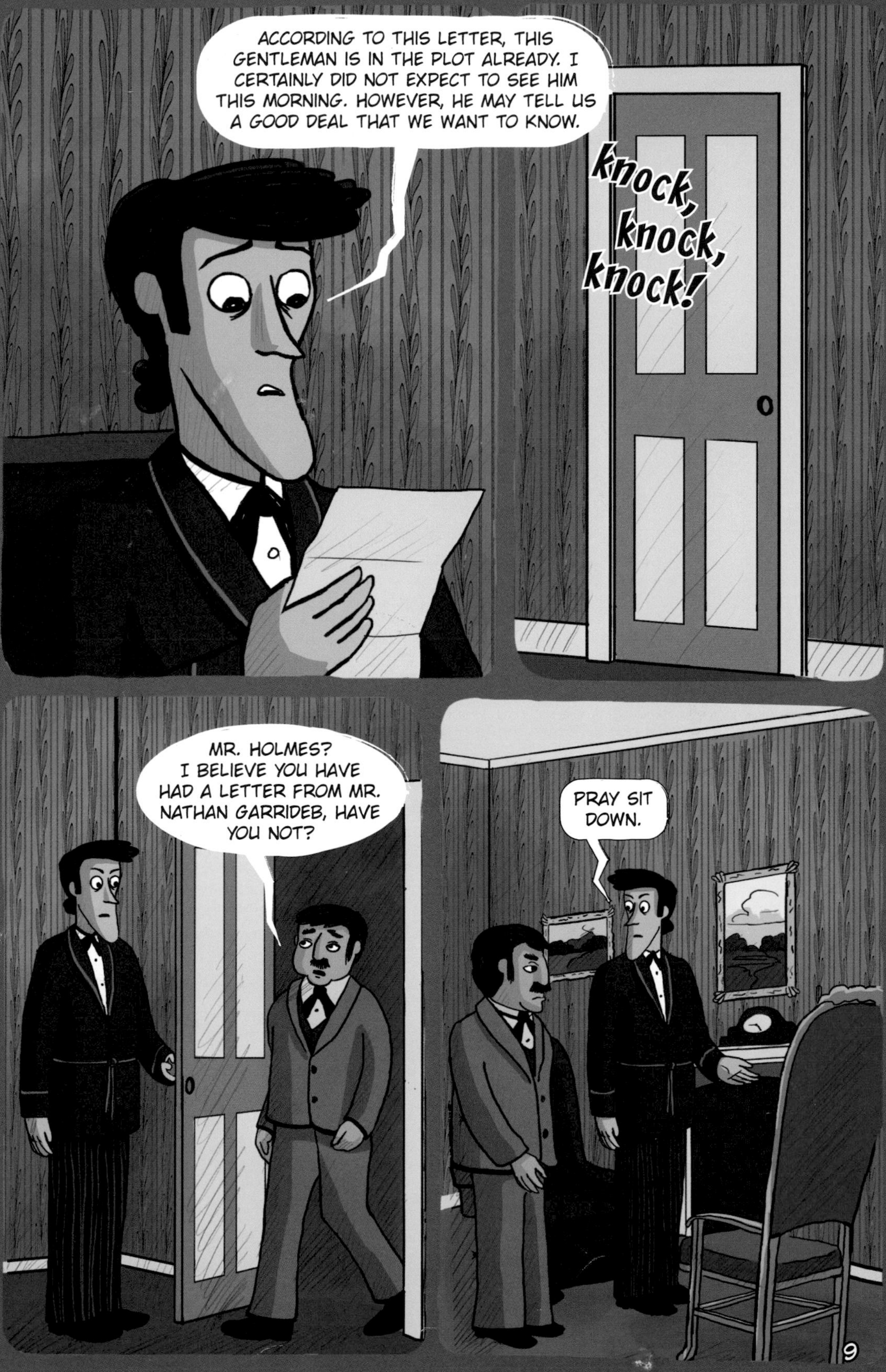
ACCORDING TO THIS LETTER, THIS GENTLEMAN IS IN THE PLOT ALREADY. I CERTAINLY DID NOT EXPECT TO SEE HIM THIS MORNING. HOWEVER, HE MAY TELL US A GOOD DEAL THAT WE WANT TO KNOW.
knock, knock, knock!
MR. HOLMES? I BELIEVE YOU HAVE HAD A LETTER FROM MR. NATHAN GARRIDEB, HAVE YOU NOT?
PRAY SIT DOWN.

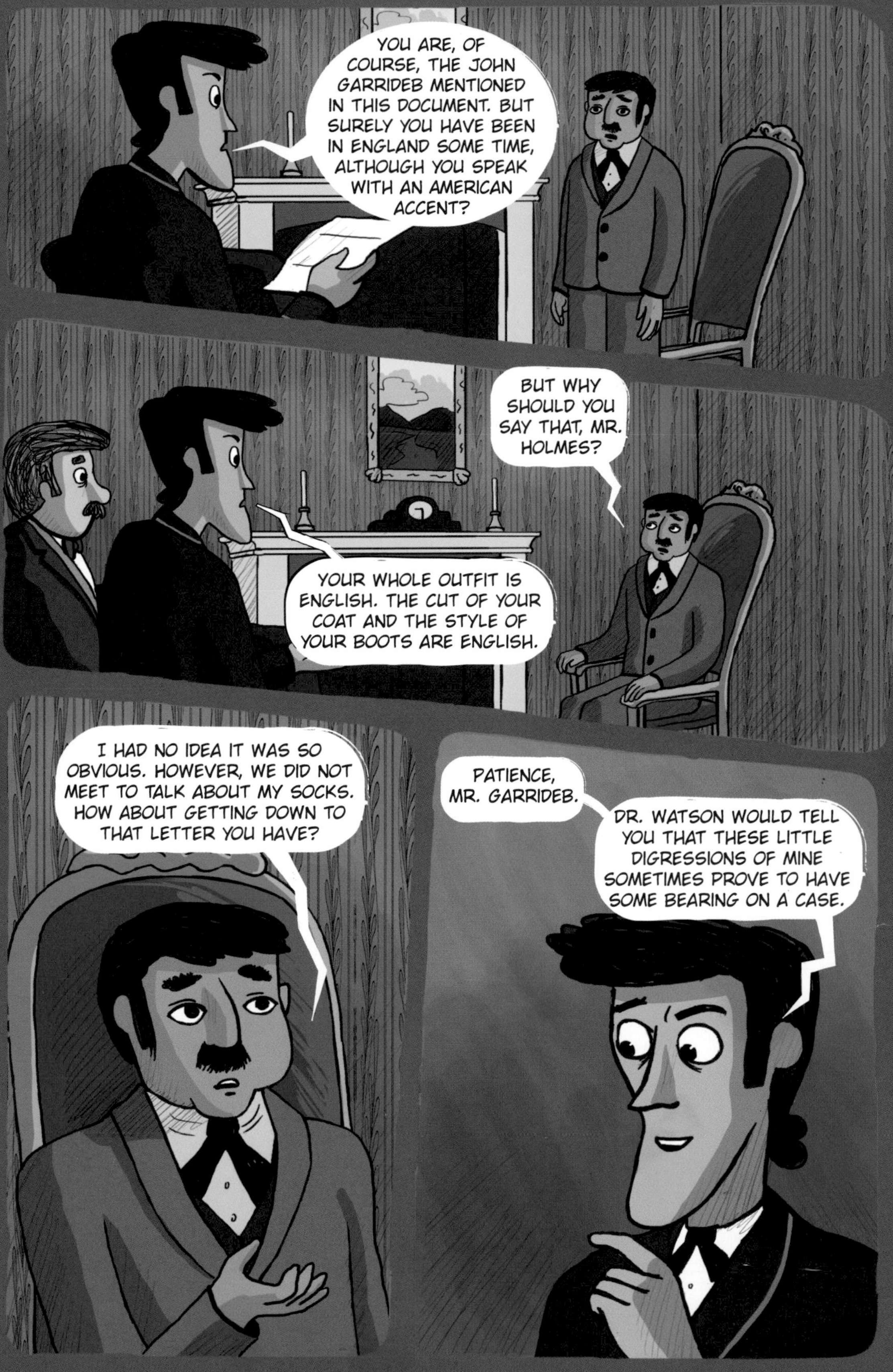
YOU ARE, OF COURSE, THE JOHN GARRIDEB MENTIONED IN THIS DOCUMENT. BUT SURELY YOU HAVE BEEN IN ENGLAND SOME TIME, ALTHOUGH YOU SPEAK WITH AN AMERICAN ACCENT?
BUT WHY SHOULD YOU SAY THAT, MR. HOLMES?
YOUR WHOLE OUTFIT IS ENGLISH. THE CUT OF YOUR COAT AND THE STYLE OF YOUR BOOTS ARE ENGLISH.
I HAD NO IDEA IT WAS SO OBVIOUS. HOWEVER, WE DID NOT MEET TO TALK ABOUT MY SOCKS. HOW ABOUT GETTING DOWN TO THAT LETTER YOU HAVE?
PATIENCE, MR. GARRIDEB.
DR. WATSON WOULD TELL YOU THAT THESE LITTLE DIGRESSIONS OF MINE SOMETIMES PROVE TO HAVE SOME BEARING ON A CASE.

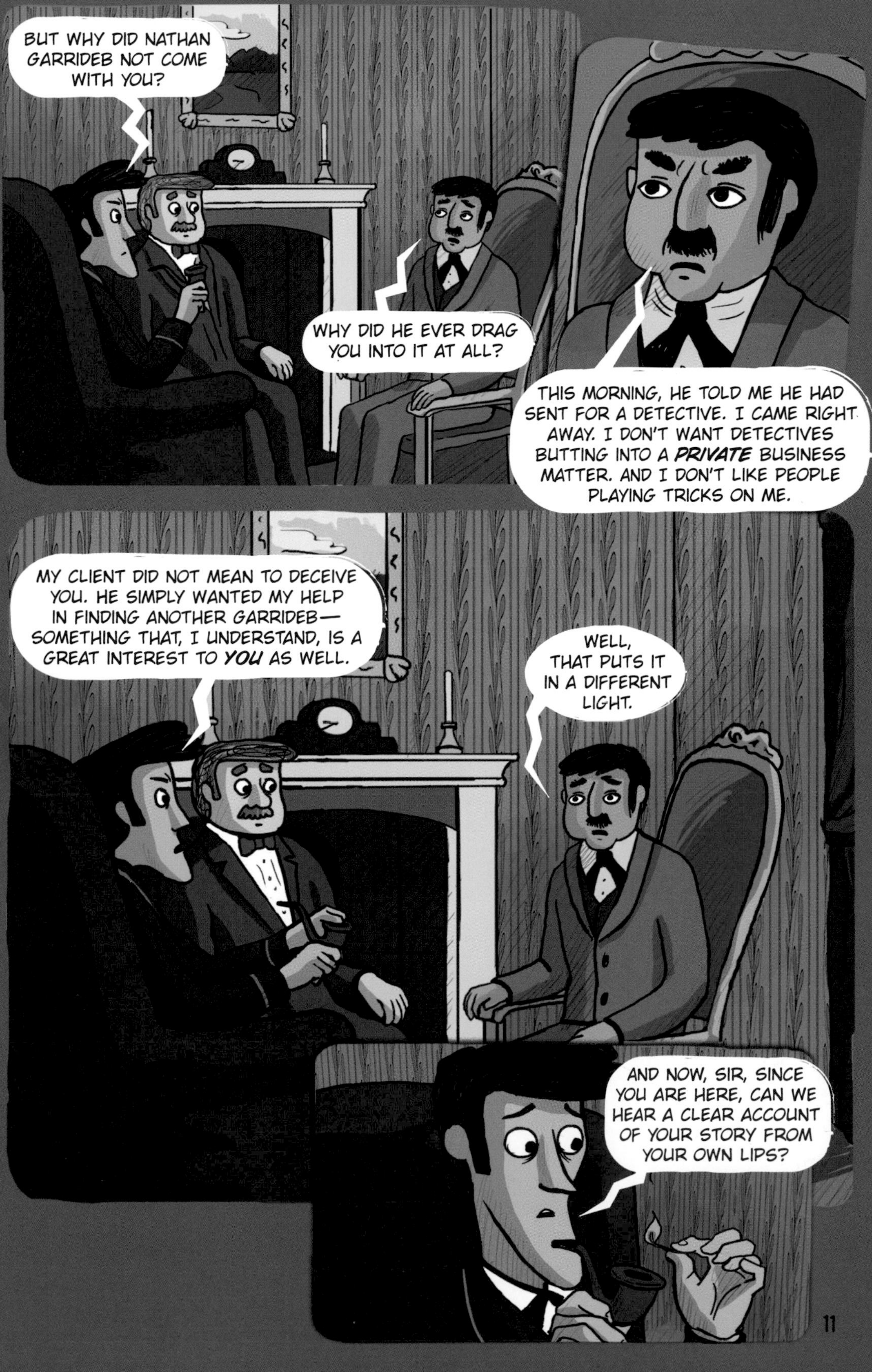
BUT WHY DID NATHAN GARRIDEB NOT COME WITH YOU?
WHY DID HE EVER DRAG YOU INTO IT AT ALL?
THIS MORNING, HE TOLD ME HE HAD SENT FOR A DETECTIVE. I CAME RIGHT AWAY. I DON'T WANT DETECTIVES BUTTING INTO A PRIVATE BUSINESS MATTER. AND I DON'T LIKE PEOPLE PLAYING TRICKS ON ME.
MY CLIENT DID NOT MEAN TO DECEIVE YOU. HE SIMPLY WANTED MY HELP IN FINDING ANOTHER GARRIDEB—SOMETHING THAT, I UNDERSTAND, IS A GREAT INTEREST TO YOU AS WELL.
WELL, THAT PUTS IT IN A DIFFERENT LIGHT.
AND NOW, SIR, SINCE YOU ARE HERE, CAN WE HEAR A CLEAR ACCOUNT OF YOUR STORY FROM YOUR OWN LIPS?

John Garrideb began by explaining that if Holmes and I were from Kansas, he would not need to explain to us who Alexander Hamilton Garrideb was. That Garrideb made his money in real estate and owned thousands of acres. He had no relatives or children, yet he wanted to leave his fortune to a Garrideb. That was what brought him to seek out John Garrideb, who was working in Topeka, Kansas, when the old gentleman visited. Alexander Hamilton Garrideb was tickled to death to meet another man with his last name.

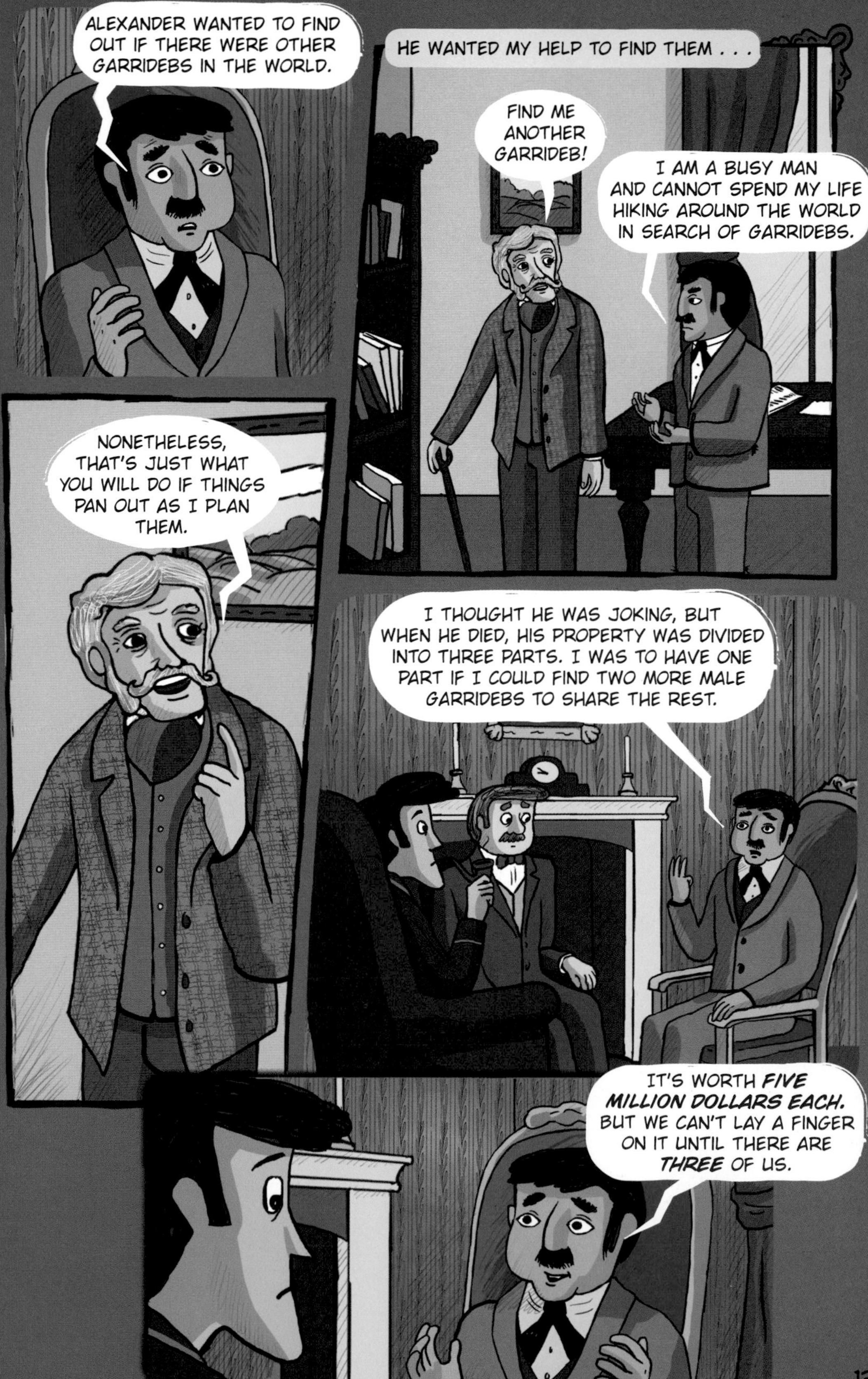
ALEXANDER WANTED TO FIND OUT IF THERE WERE OTHER GARRIDEBS IN THE WORLD.
HE WANTED MY HELP TO FIND THEM . . .
FIND ME ANOTHER GARRIDEB!
I AM A BUSY MAN AND CANNOT SPEND MY LIFE HIKING AROUND THE WORLD IN SEARCH OF GARRIDEBS.
NONETHELESS, THAT'S JUST WHAT YOU WILL DO IF THINGS PAN OUT AS I PLAN THEM.
I THOUGHT HE WAS JOKING, BUT WHEN HE DIED, HIS PROPERTY WAS DIVIDED INTO THREE PARTS. I WAS TO HAVE ONE PART IF I COULD FIND TWO MORE MALE GARRIDEBS TO SHARE THE REST.
IT'S WORTH ***FIVE MILLION DOLLARS EACH.*** BUT WE CAN'T LAY A FINGER ON IT UNTIL THERE ARE ***THREE*** OF US.

Our visitor explained that he had left his job and started looking for Garridebs. There was not another one in the United States. He went through the country with a fine-tooth comb, and never a Garrideb could he find. Then, he tried England. Sure enough, there was a name in the London telephone directory. He went after Nathan Garrideb two days ago and explained the whole matter to him. But like John Garrideb, Nathan is the only man left in his family. It states in the will that there must be three adult men. The two Garridebs had advertised in the papers but had no reply yet. John Garrideb told us that if we could help them find a third Garrideb, he and Nathan would pay our charges.

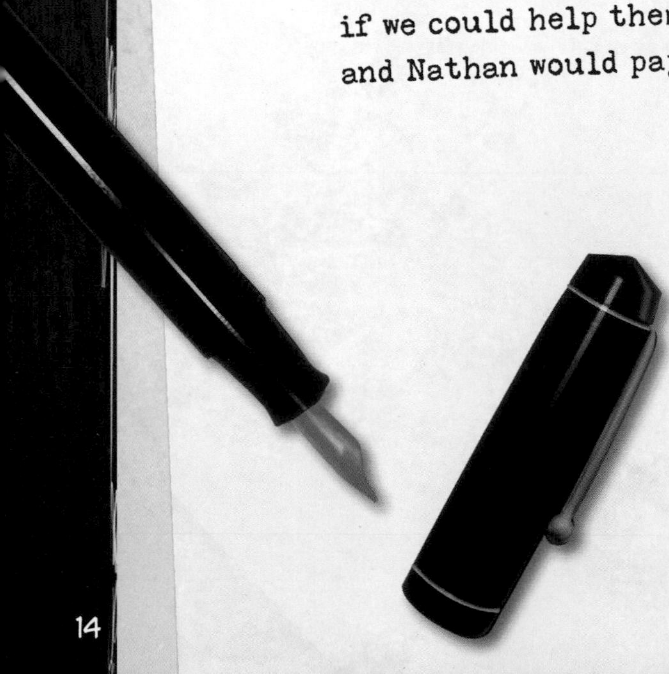

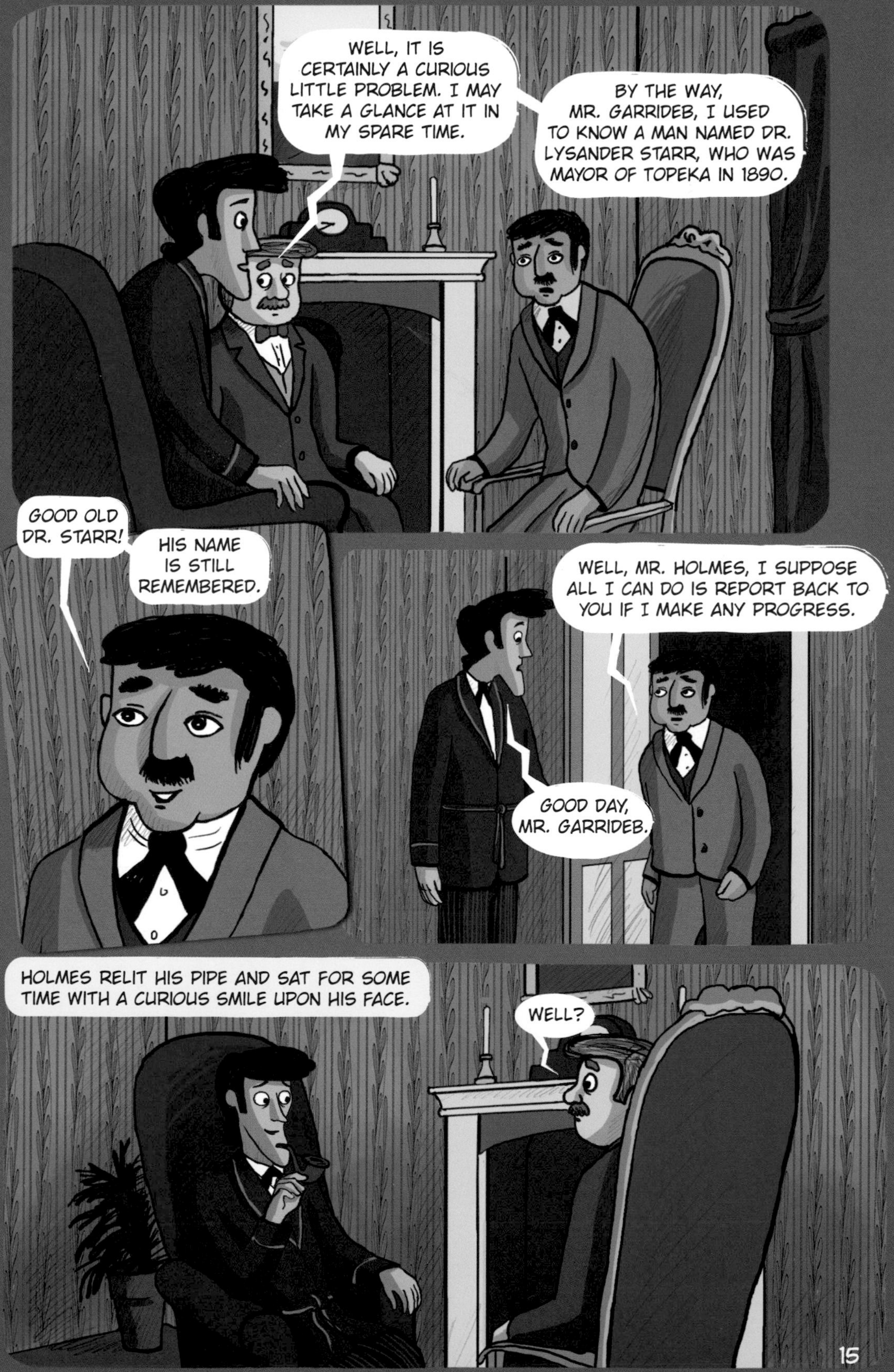
WELL, IT IS CERTAINLY A CURIOUS LITTLE PROBLEM. I MAY TAKE A GLANCE AT IT IN MY SPARE TIME.
BY THE WAY, MR. GARRIDEB, I USED TO KNOW A MAN NAMED DR. LYSANDER STARR, WHO WAS MAYOR OF TOPEKA IN 1890.
GOOD OLD DR. STARR!
HIS NAME IS STILL REMEMBERED.
WELL, MR. HOLMES, I SUPPOSE ALL I CAN DO IS REPORT BACK TO YOU IF I MAKE ANY PROGRESS.
GOOD DAY, MR. GARRIDEB.
HOLMES RELIT HIS PIPE AND SAT FOR SOME TIME WITH A CURIOUS SMILE UPON HIS FACE.
WELL?

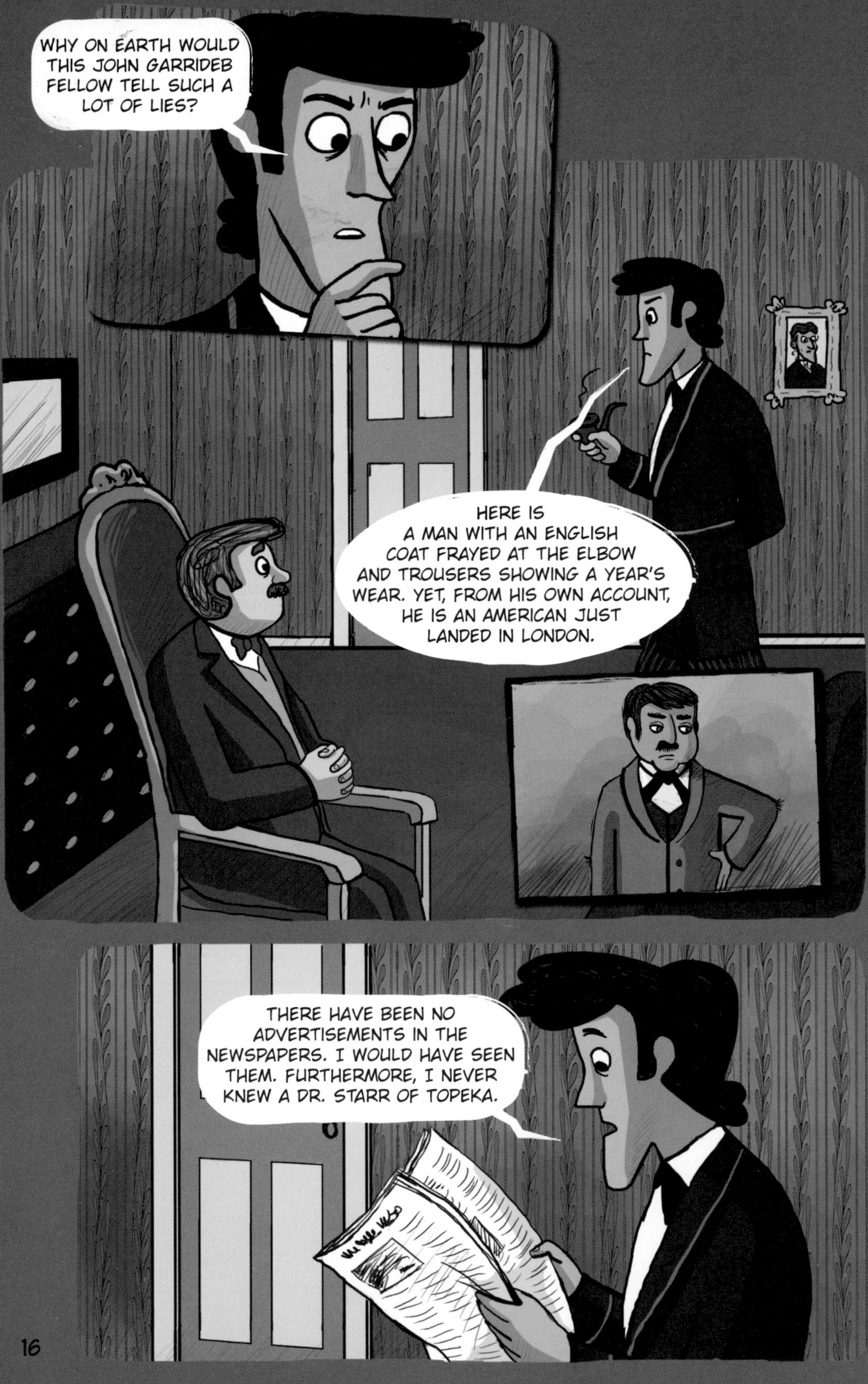
WHY ON EARTH WOULD THIS JOHN GARRIDEB FELLOW TELL SUCH A LOT OF LIES?
HERE IS A MAN WITH AN ENGLISH COAT FRAYED AT THE ELBOW AND TROUSERS SHOWING A YEAR'S WEAR. YET, FROM HIS OWN ACCOUNT, HE IS AN AMERICAN JUST LANDED IN LONDON.
THERE HAVE BEEN NO ADVERTISEMENTS IN THE NEWSPAPERS. I WOULD HAVE SEEN THEM. FURTHERMORE, I NEVER KNEW A DR. STARR OF TOPEKA.

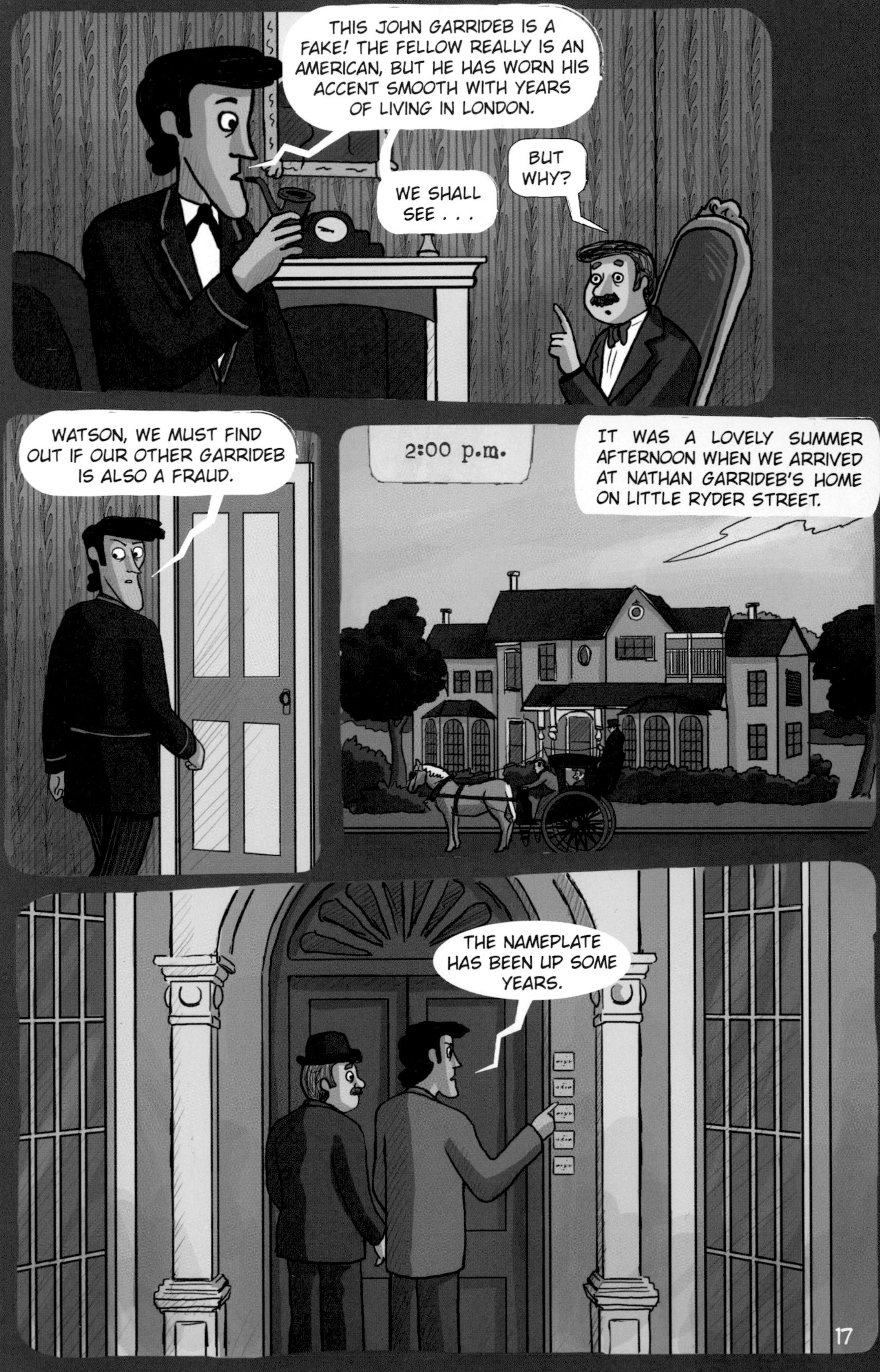
THIS JOHN GARRIDEB IS A FAKE! THE FELLOW REALLY IS AN AMERICAN, BUT HE HAS WORN HIS ACCENT SMOOTH WITH YEARS OF LIVING IN LONDON.
BUT WHY?
WE SHALL SEE . . .
WATSON, WE MUST FIND OUT IF OUR OTHER GARRIDEB IS ALSO A FRAUD.
2:00 p.m.
IT WAS A LOVELY SUMMER AFTERNOON WHEN WE ARRIVED AT NATHAN GARRIDEB'S HOME ON LITTLE RYDER STREET.
THE NAMEPLATE HAS BEEN UP SOME YEARS.

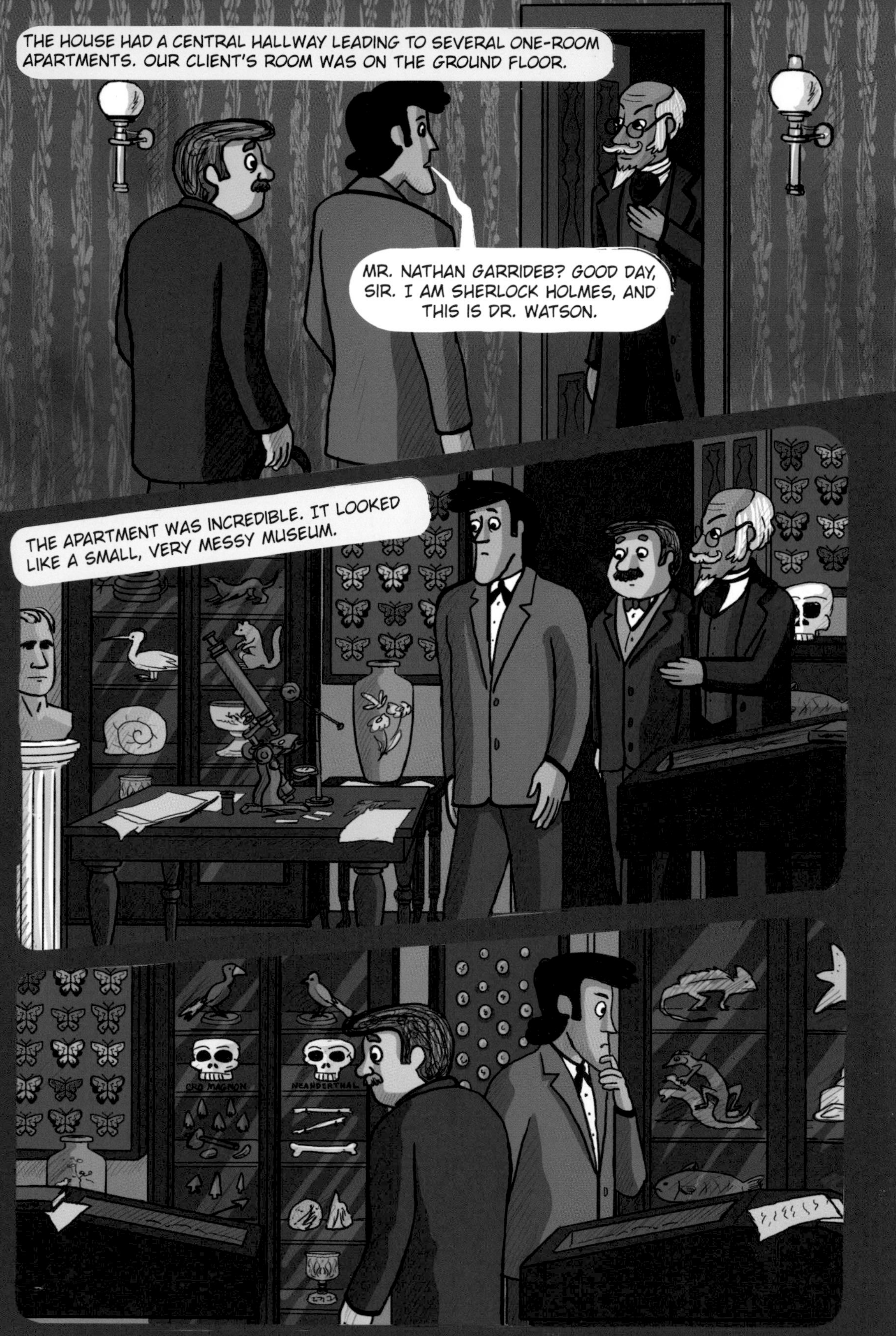
THE HOUSE HAD A CENTRAL HALLWAY LEADING TO SEVERAL ONE-ROOM APARTMENTS. OUR CLIENT'S ROOM WAS ON THE GROUND FLOOR.
MR. NATHAN GARRIDEB? GOOD DAY, SIR. I AM SHERLOCK HOLMES, AND THIS IS DR. WATSON.
THE APARTMENT WAS INCREDIBLE. IT LOOKED LIKE A SMALL, VERY MESSY MUSEUM.
CRO MAGNON
NEANDERTHAL

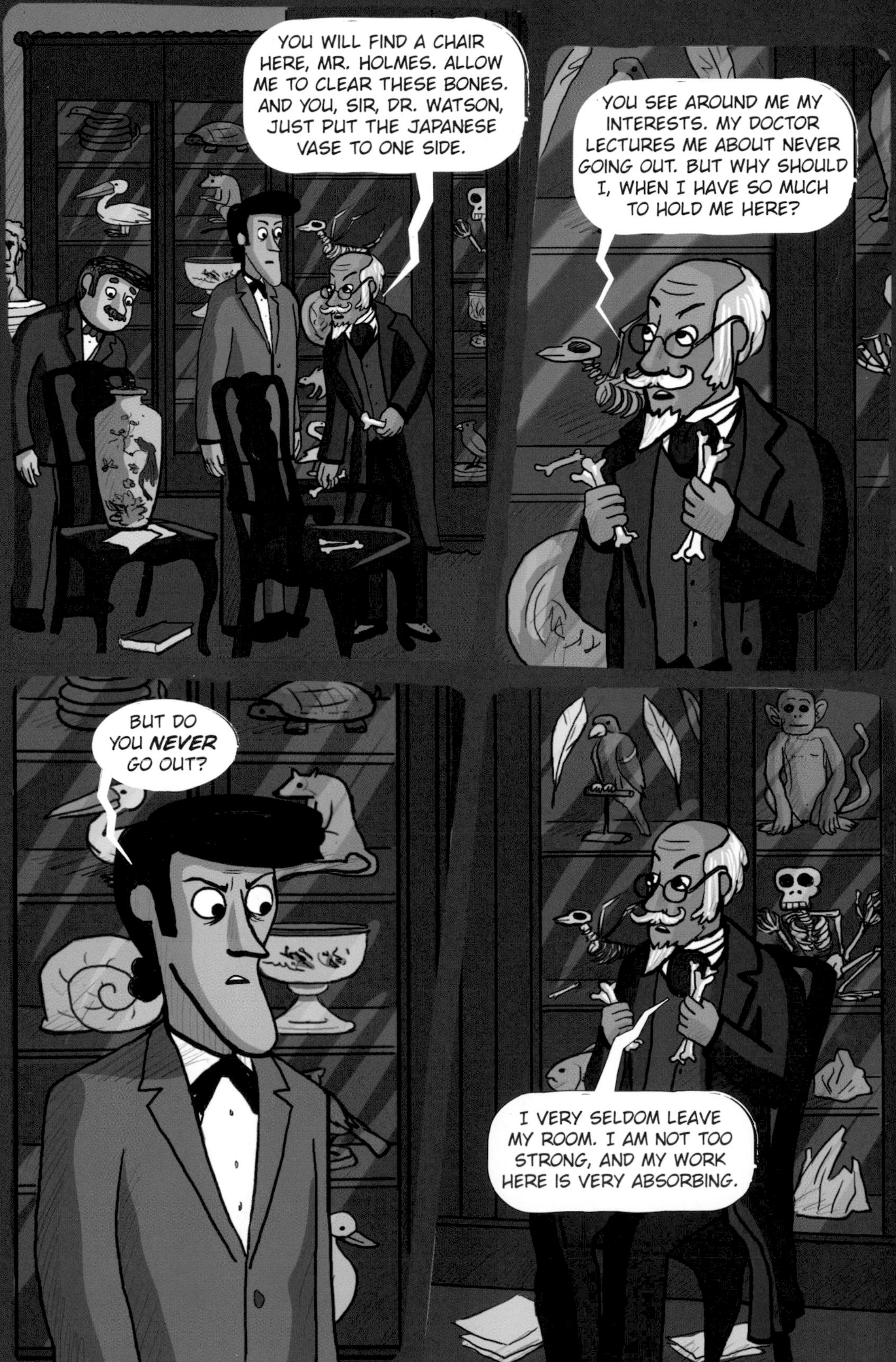
YOU WILL FIND A CHAIR HERE, MR. HOLMES. ALLOW ME TO CLEAR THESE BONES. AND YOU, SIR, DR. WATSON, JUST PUT THE JAPANESE VASE TO ONE SIDE.
YOU SEE AROUND ME MY INTERESTS. MY DOCTOR LECTURES ME ABOUT NEVER GOING OUT. BUT WHY SHOULD I, WHEN I HAVE SO MUCH TO HOLD ME HERE?
BUT DO YOU ***NEVER*** GO OUT?
I VERY SELDOM LEAVE MY ROOM. I AM NOT TOO STRONG, AND MY WORK HERE IS VERY ABSORBING.

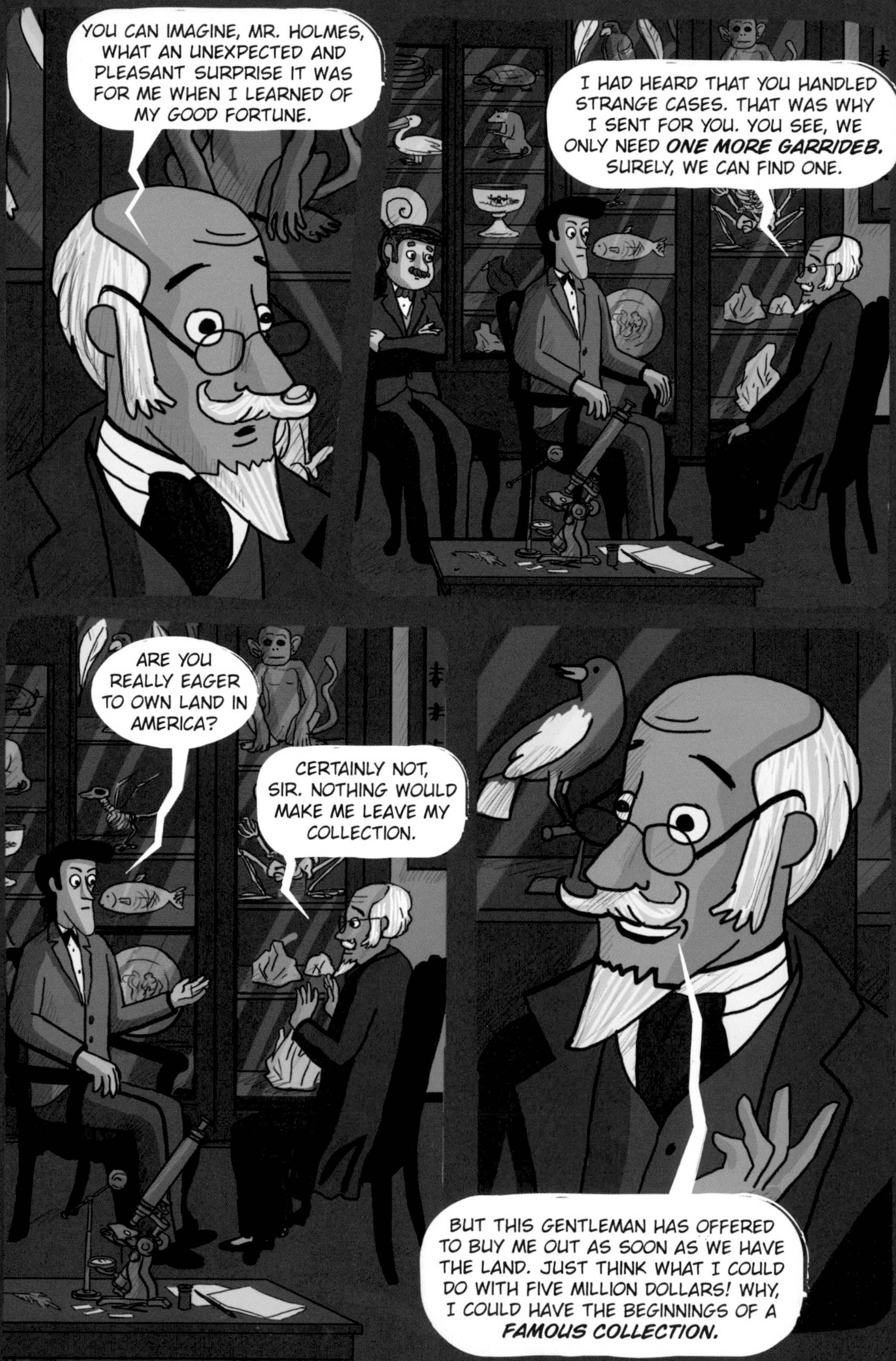

YOU CAN IMAGINE, MR. HOLMES, WHAT AN UNEXPECTED AND PLEASANT SURPRISE IT WAS FOR ME WHEN I LEARNED OF MY GOOD FORTUNE.
I HAD HEARD THAT YOU HANDLED STRANGE CASES. THAT WAS WHY I SENT FOR YOU. YOU SEE, WE ONLY NEED ***ONE MORE GARRIDEB.*** SURELY, WE CAN FIND ONE.
ARE YOU REALLY EAGER TO OWN LAND IN AMERICA?
CERTAINLY NOT, SIR. NOTHING WOULD MAKE ME LEAVE MY COLLECTION.
BUT THIS GENTLEMAN HAS OFFERED TO BUY ME OUT AS SOON AS WE HAVE THE LAND. JUST THINK WHAT I COULD DO WITH FIVE MILLION DOLLARS! WHY, I COULD HAVE THE BEGINNINGS OF A ***FAMOUS COLLECTION.***

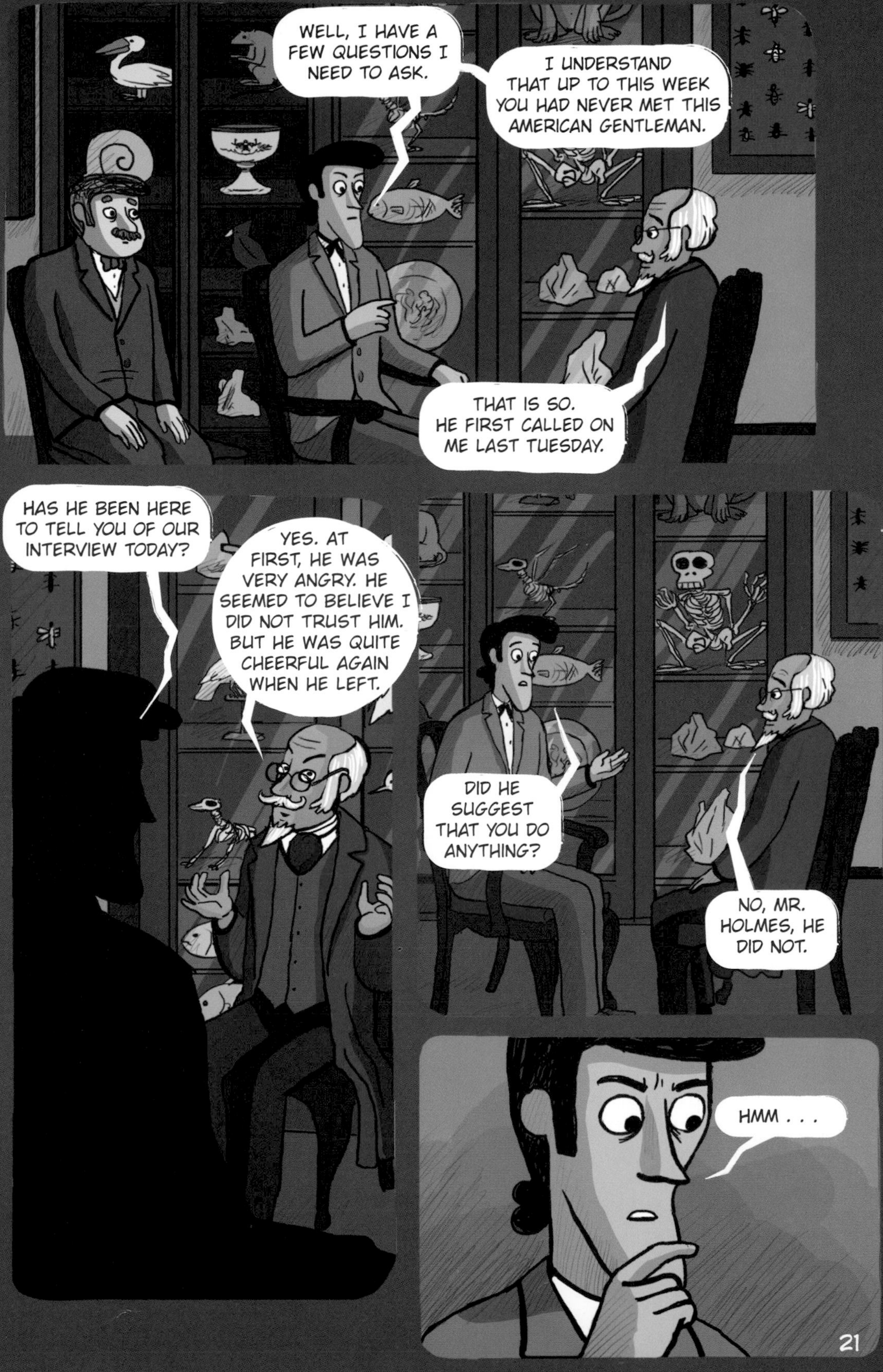
WELL, I HAVE A FEW QUESTIONS I NEED TO ASK.
I UNDERSTAND THAT UP TO THIS WEEK YOU HAD NEVER MET THIS AMERICAN GENTLEMAN.
THAT IS SO. HE FIRST CALLED ON ME LAST TUESDAY.
HAS HE BEEN HERE TO TELL YOU OF OUR INTERVIEW TODAY?
YES. AT FIRST, HE WAS VERY ANGRY. HE SEEMED TO BELIEVE I DID NOT TRUST HIM. BUT HE WAS QUITE CHEERFUL AGAIN WHEN HE LEFT.
DID HE SUGGEST THAT YOU DO ANYTHING?
NO, MR. HOLMES, HE DID NOT.
HMM . . .

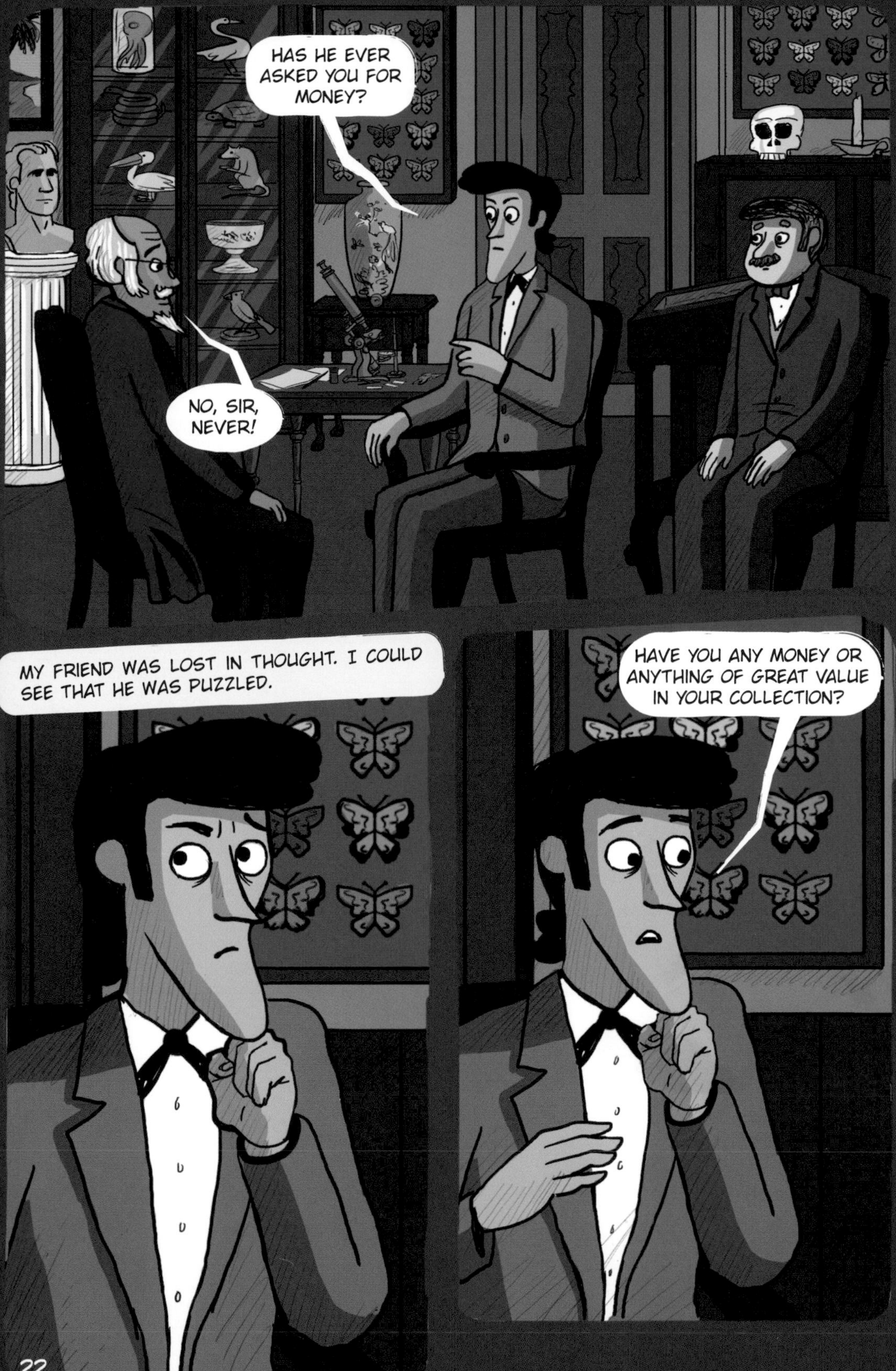
HAS HE EVER ASKED YOU FOR MONEY?
NO, SIR, NEVER!
MY FRIEND WAS LOST IN THOUGHT. I COULD SEE THAT HE WAS PUZZLED.
HAVE YOU ANY MONEY OR ANYTHING OF GREAT VALUE IN YOUR COLLECTION?

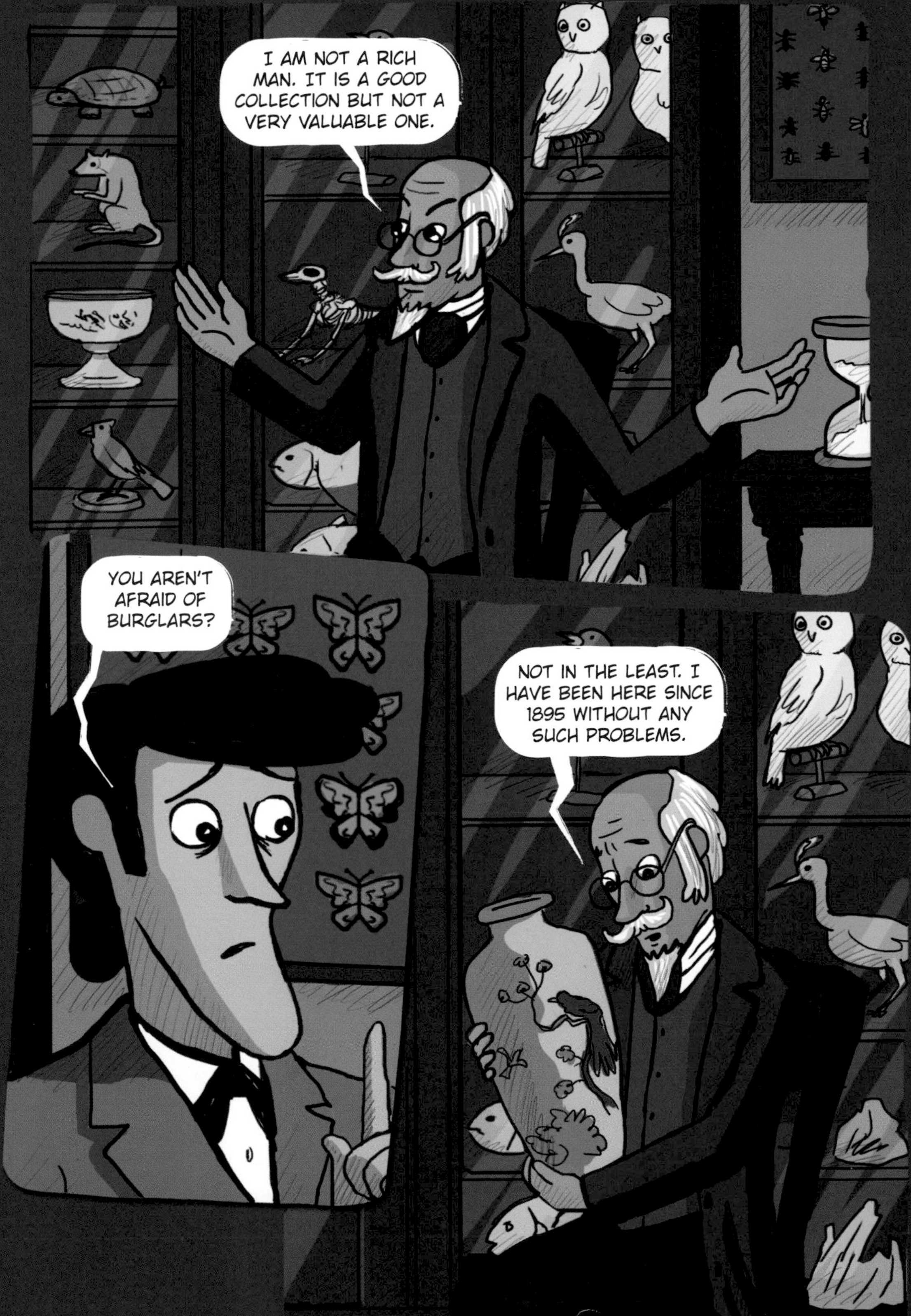
I AM NOT A RICH MAN. IT IS A GOOD COLLECTION BUT NOT A VERY VALUABLE ONE.
YOU AREN'T AFRAID OF BURGLARS?
NOT IN THE LEAST. I HAVE BEEN HERE SINCE 1895 WITHOUT ANY SUCH PROBLEMS.

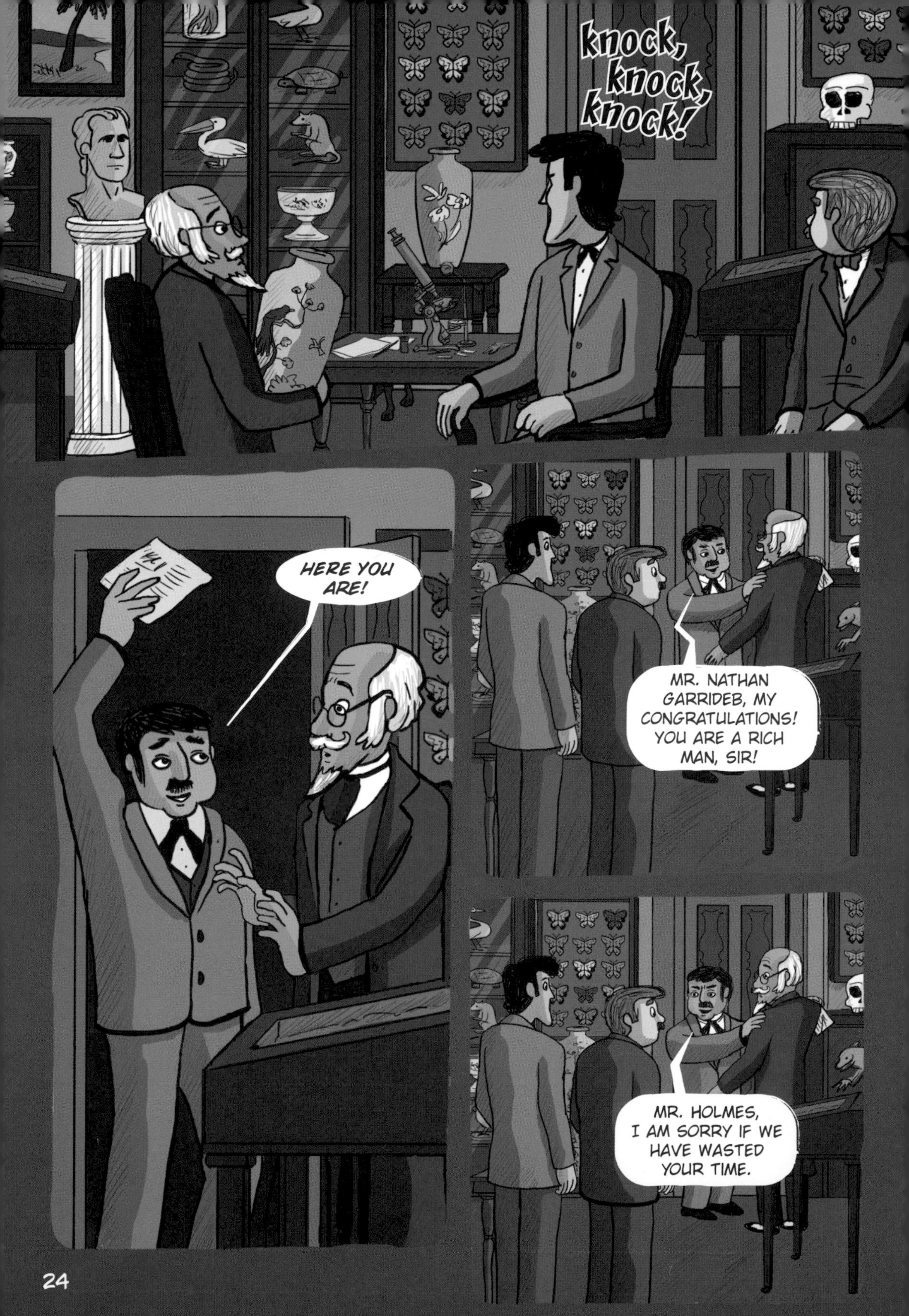
knock, knock, knock!
HERE YOU ARE!
MR. NATHAN GARRIDEB, MY CONGRATULATIONS! YOU ARE A RICH MAN, SIR!
MR. HOLMES, I AM SORRY IF WE HAVE WASTED YOUR TIME.

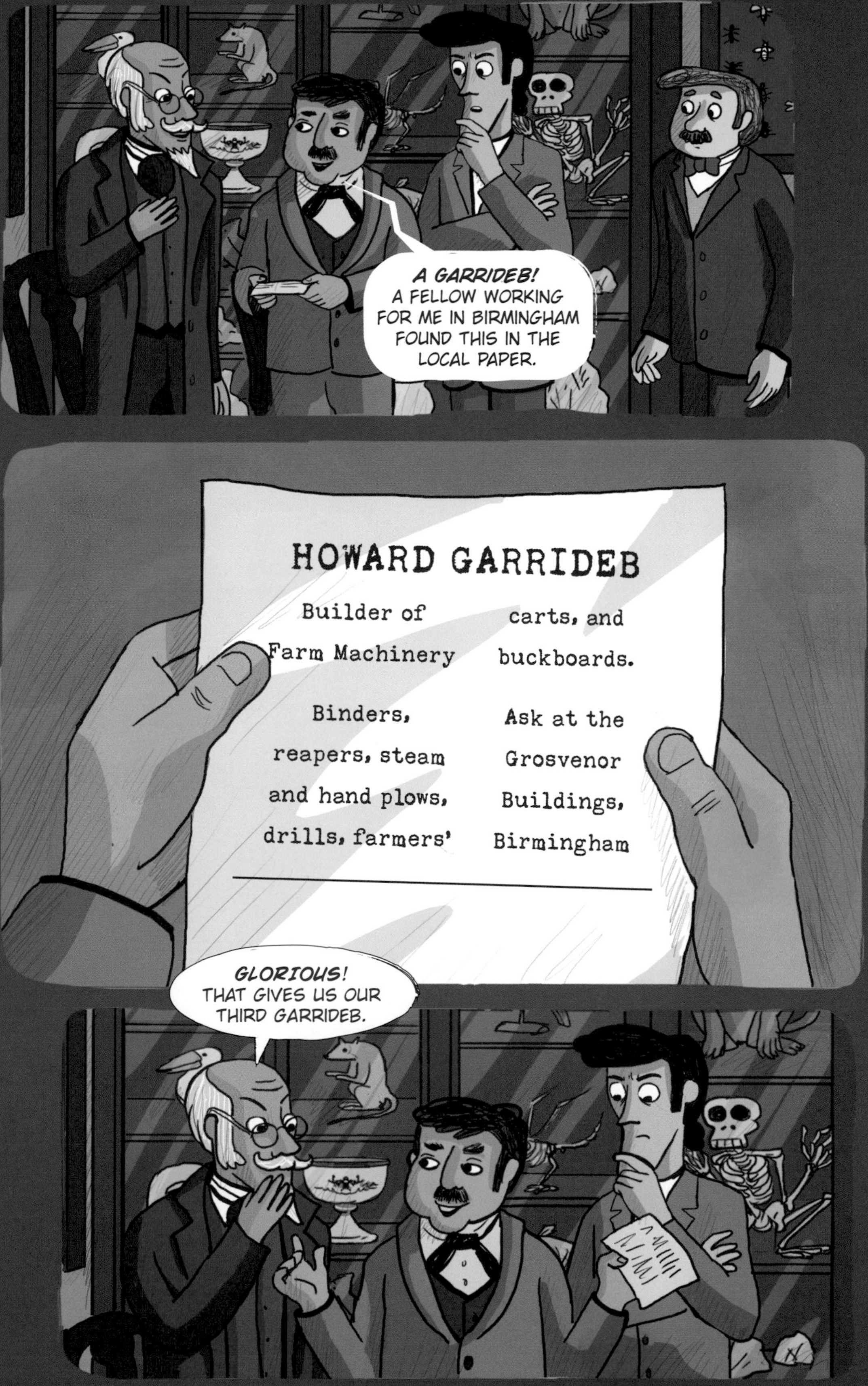
A GARRIDEB! A FELLOW WORKING FOR ME IN BIRMINGHAM FOUND THIS IN THE LOCAL PAPER.
HOWARD GARRIDEB
Builder of Farm Machinery
Binders, reapers, steam and hand plows, drills, farmers' carts, and buckboards.
Ask at the Grosvenor Buildings, Birmingham
GLORIOUS! THAT GIVES US OUR THIRD GARRIDEB.

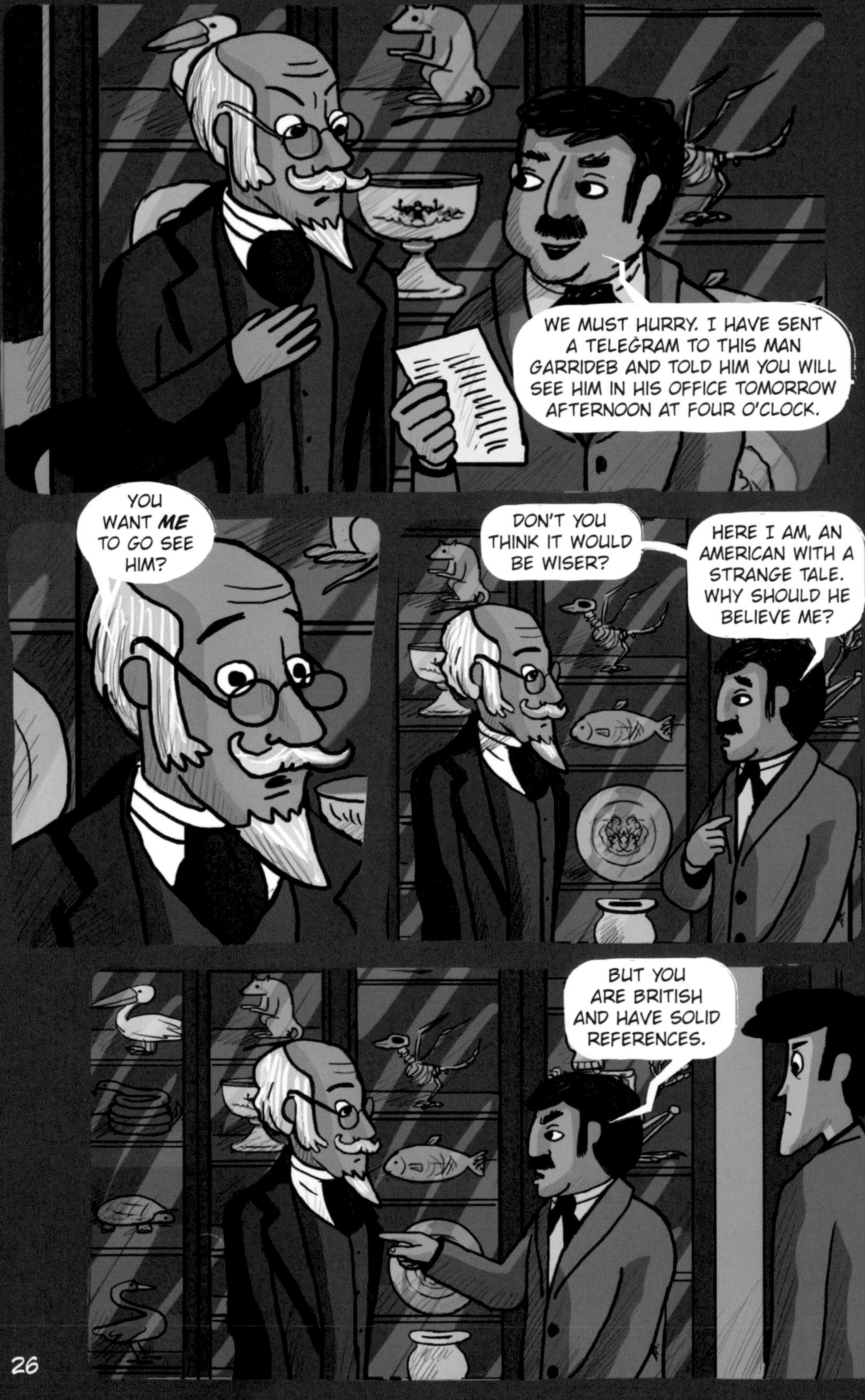
WE MUST HURRY. I HAVE SENT A TELEGRAM TO THIS MAN GARRIDEB AND TOLD HIM YOU WILL SEE HIM IN HIS OFFICE TOMORROW AFTERNOON AT FOUR O'CLOCK.
YOU WANT *ME* TO GO SEE HIM?
DON'T YOU THINK IT WOULD BE WISER?
HERE I AM, AN AMERICAN WITH A STRANGE TALE. WHY SHOULD HE BELIEVE ME?
BUT YOU ARE BRITISH AND HAVE SOLID REFERENCES.

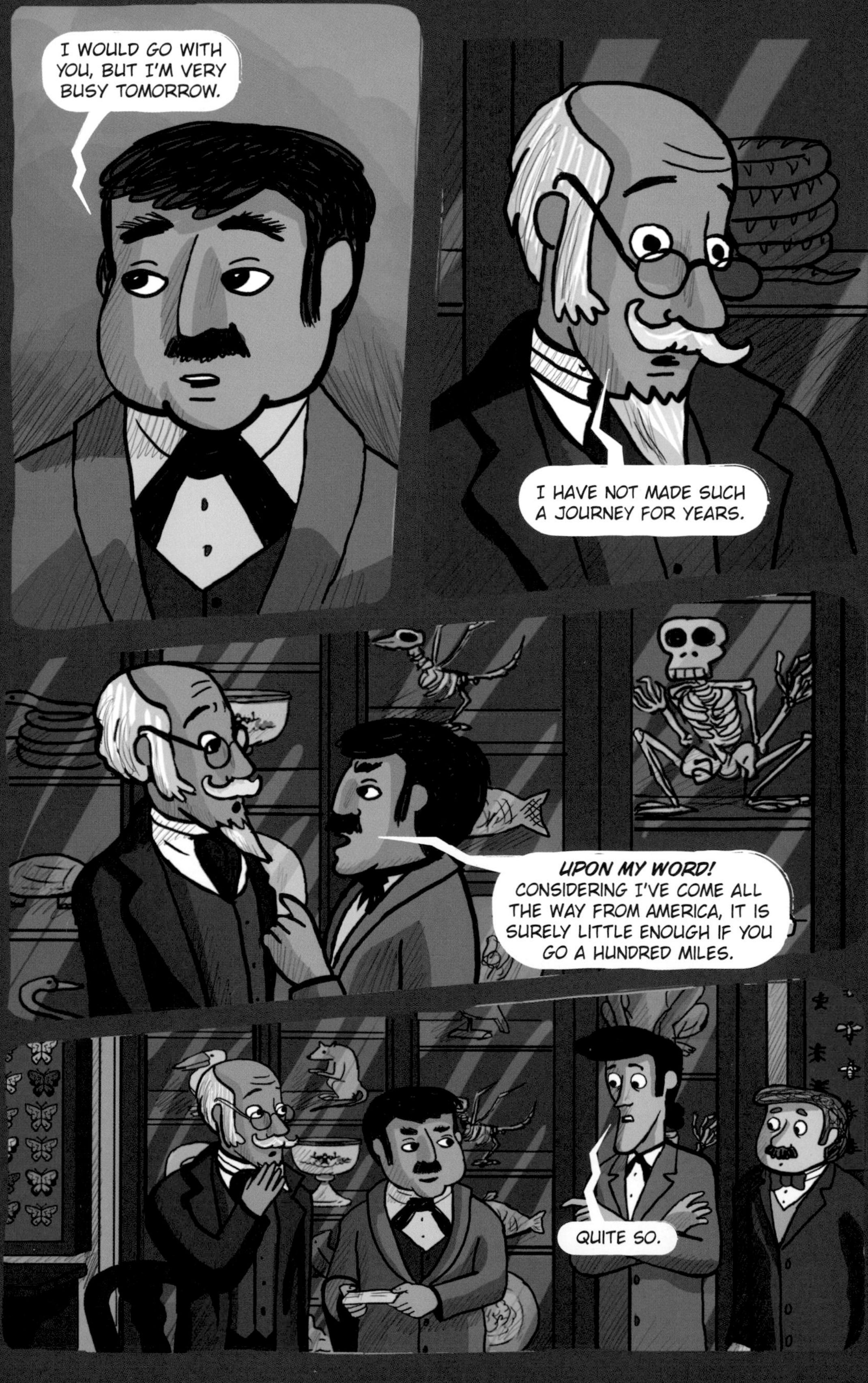
I WOULD GO WITH YOU, BUT I'M VERY BUSY TOMORROW.
I HAVE NOT MADE SUCH A JOURNEY FOR YEARS.
UPON MY WORD! CONSIDERING I'VE COME ALL THE WAY FROM AMERICA, IT IS SURELY LITTLE ENOUGH IF YOU GO A HUNDRED MILES.
QUITE SO.

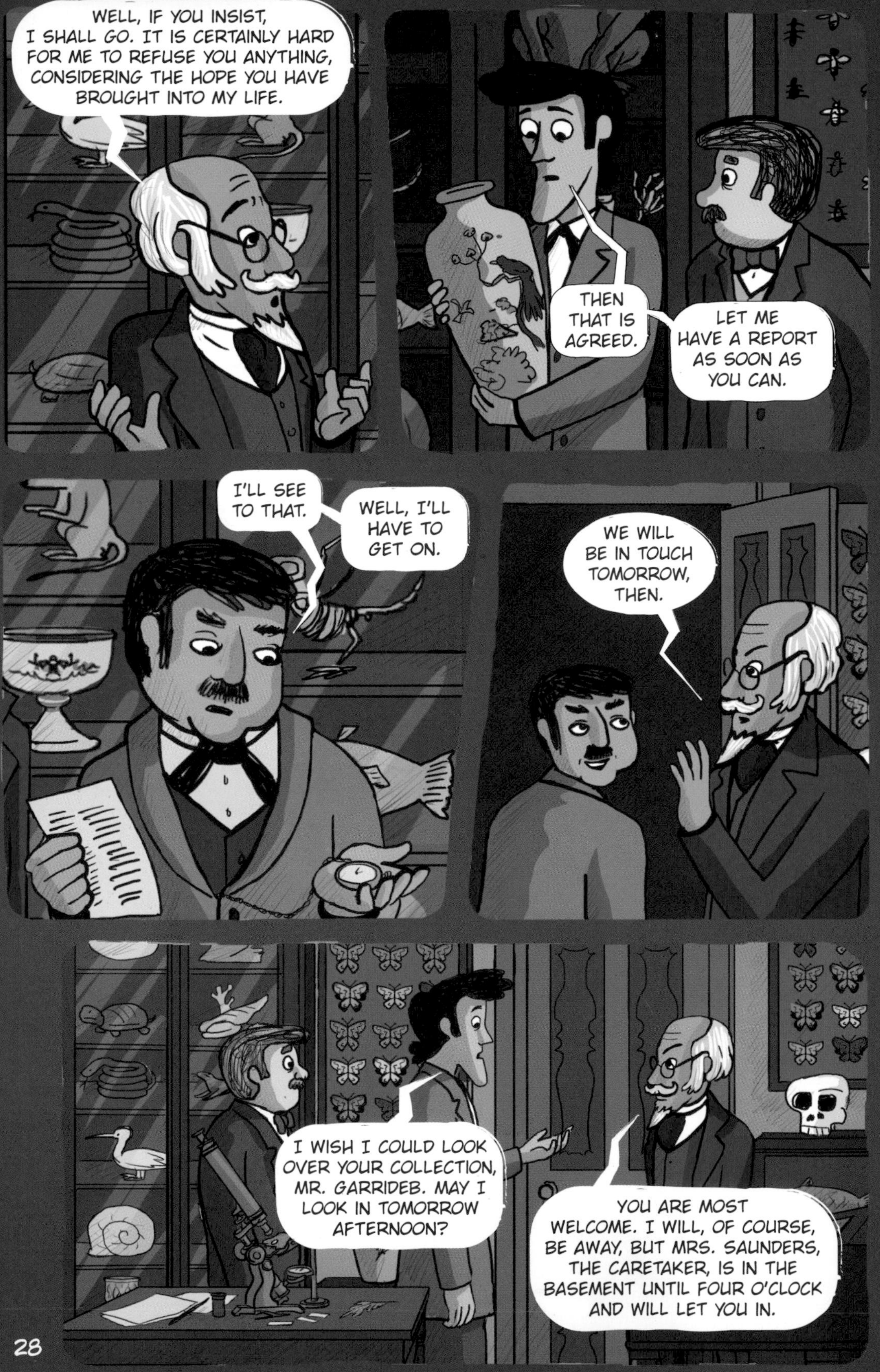
WELL, IF YOU INSIST, I SHALL GO. IT IS CERTAINLY HARD FOR ME TO REFUSE YOU ANYTHING, CONSIDERING THE HOPE YOU HAVE BROUGHT INTO MY LIFE.
THEN THAT IS AGREED.
LET ME HAVE A REPORT AS SOON AS YOU CAN.
I'LL SEE TO THAT.
WELL, I'LL HAVE TO GET ON.
WE WILL BE IN TOUCH TOMORROW, THEN.
I WISH I COULD LOOK OVER YOUR COLLECTION, MR. GARRIDEB. MAY I LOOK IN TOMORROW AFTERNOON?
YOU ARE MOST WELCOME. I WILL, OF COURSE, BE AWAY, BUT MRS. SAUNDERS, THE CARETAKER, IS IN THE BASEMENT UNTIL FOUR O'CLOCK AND WILL LET YOU IN.

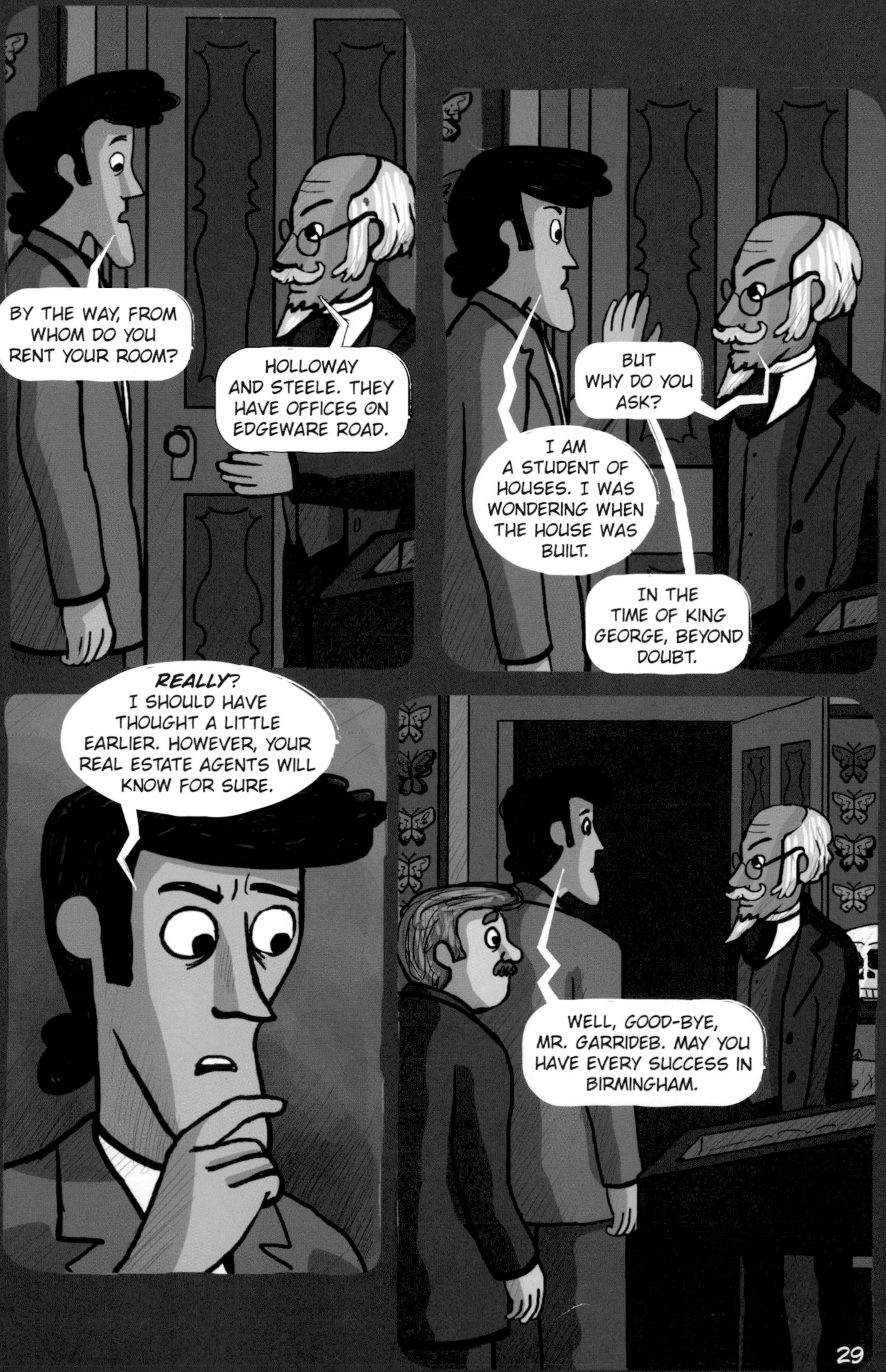

BY THE WAY, FROM WHOM DO YOU RENT YOUR ROOM?
HOLLOWAY AND STEELE. THEY HAVE OFFICES ON EDGEWARE ROAD.
BUT WHY DO YOU ASK?
I AM A STUDENT OF HOUSES. I WAS WONDERING WHEN THE HOUSE WAS BUILT.
IN THE TIME OF KING GEORGE, BEYOND DOUBT.
REALLY? I SHOULD HAVE THOUGHT A LITTLE EARLIER. HOWEVER, YOUR REAL ESTATE AGENTS WILL KNOW FOR SURE.
WELL, GOOD-BYE, MR. GARRIDEB. MAY YOU HAVE EVERY SUCCESS IN BIRMINGHAM.

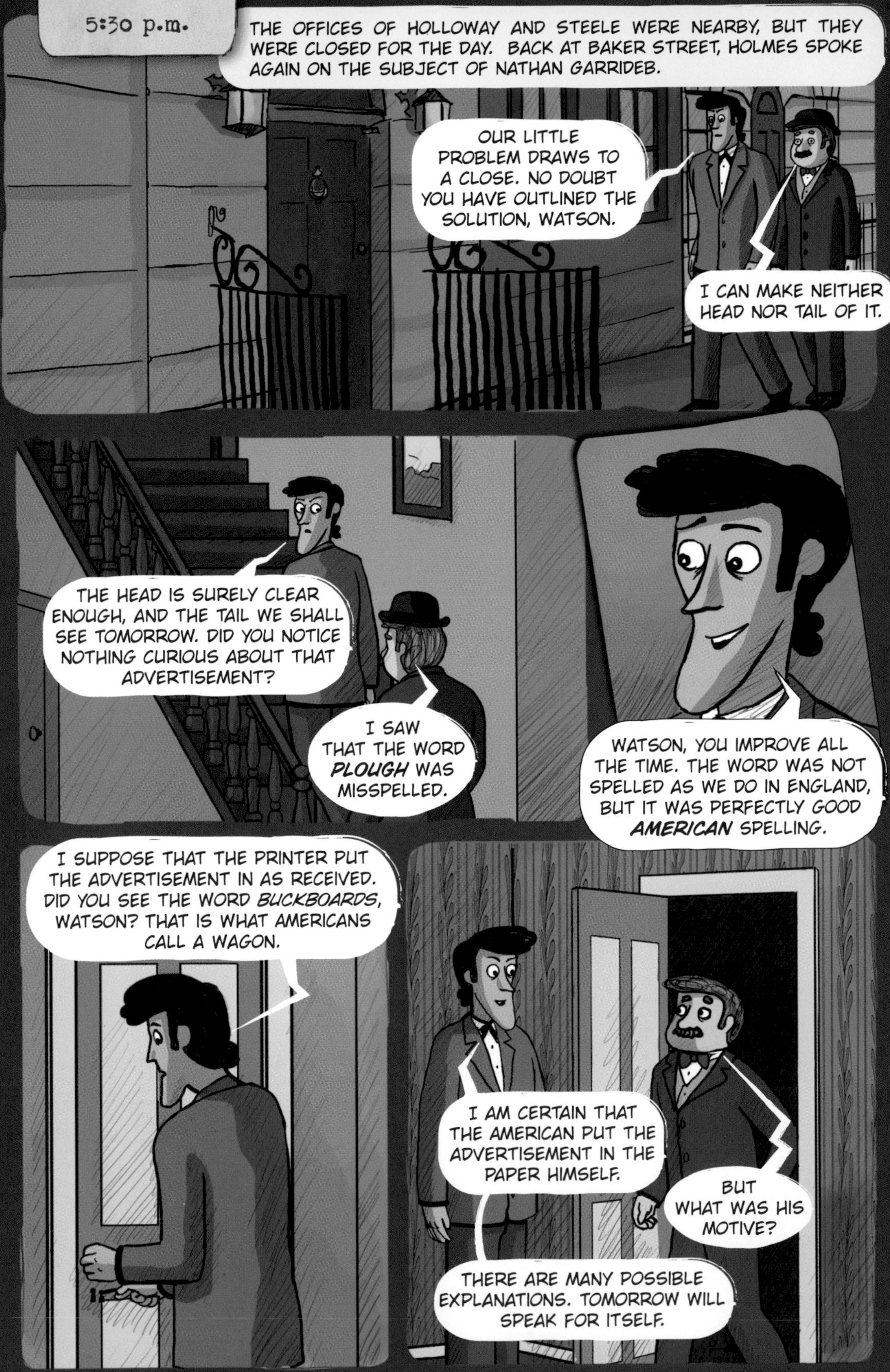
5:30 p.m.
THE OFFICES OF HOLLOWAY AND STEELE WERE NEARBY, BUT THEY WERE CLOSED FOR THE DAY. BACK AT BAKER STREET, HOLMES SPOKE AGAIN ON THE SUBJECT OF NATHAN GARRIDEB.
OUR LITTLE PROBLEM DRAWS TO A CLOSE. NO DOUBT YOU HAVE OUTLINED THE SOLUTION, WATSON.
I CAN MAKE NEITHER HEAD NOR TAIL OF IT.
THE HEAD IS SURELY CLEAR ENOUGH, AND THE TAIL WE SHALL SEE TOMORROW. DID YOU NOTICE NOTHING CURIOUS ABOUT THAT ADVERTISEMENT?
I SAW THAT THE WORD *PLOUGH* WAS MISSPELLED.
WATSON, YOU IMPROVE ALL THE TIME. THE WORD WAS NOT SPELLED AS WE DO IN ENGLAND, BUT IT WAS PERFECTLY GOOD **AMERICAN** SPELLING.
I SUPPOSE THAT THE PRINTER PUT THE ADVERTISEMENT IN AS RECEIVED. DID YOU SEE THE WORD *BUCKBOARDS*, WATSON? THAT IS WHAT AMERICANS CALL A WAGON.
I AM CERTAIN THAT THE AMERICAN PUT THE ADVERTISEMENT IN THE PAPER HIMSELF.
BUT WHAT WAS HIS MOTIVE?
THERE ARE MANY POSSIBLE EXPLANATIONS. TOMORROW WILL SPEAK FOR ITSELF.

June 24, 1902

Holmes was up and out early the next day. When he returned at lunchtime, his face was very grave. He explained that the case was far more serious than he had expected. He had been to Scotland Yard and had found that our American friend was in their photographic records. Holmes read the following from his notes: "James Winter, alias Morecroft, alias Killer Evans. Aged forty-four. Native of Chicago. Came to London in 1893. Shot a man in an argument in January 1895. Man died and was identified as Roger Prescott, a famous maker of counterfeit money. Evans was sent to jail but recently escaped. Very dangerous man. Known to carry a gun and prepared to use it."

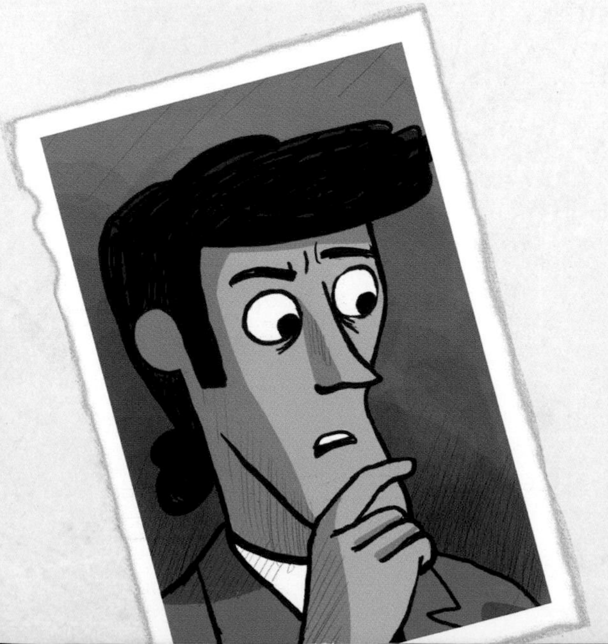

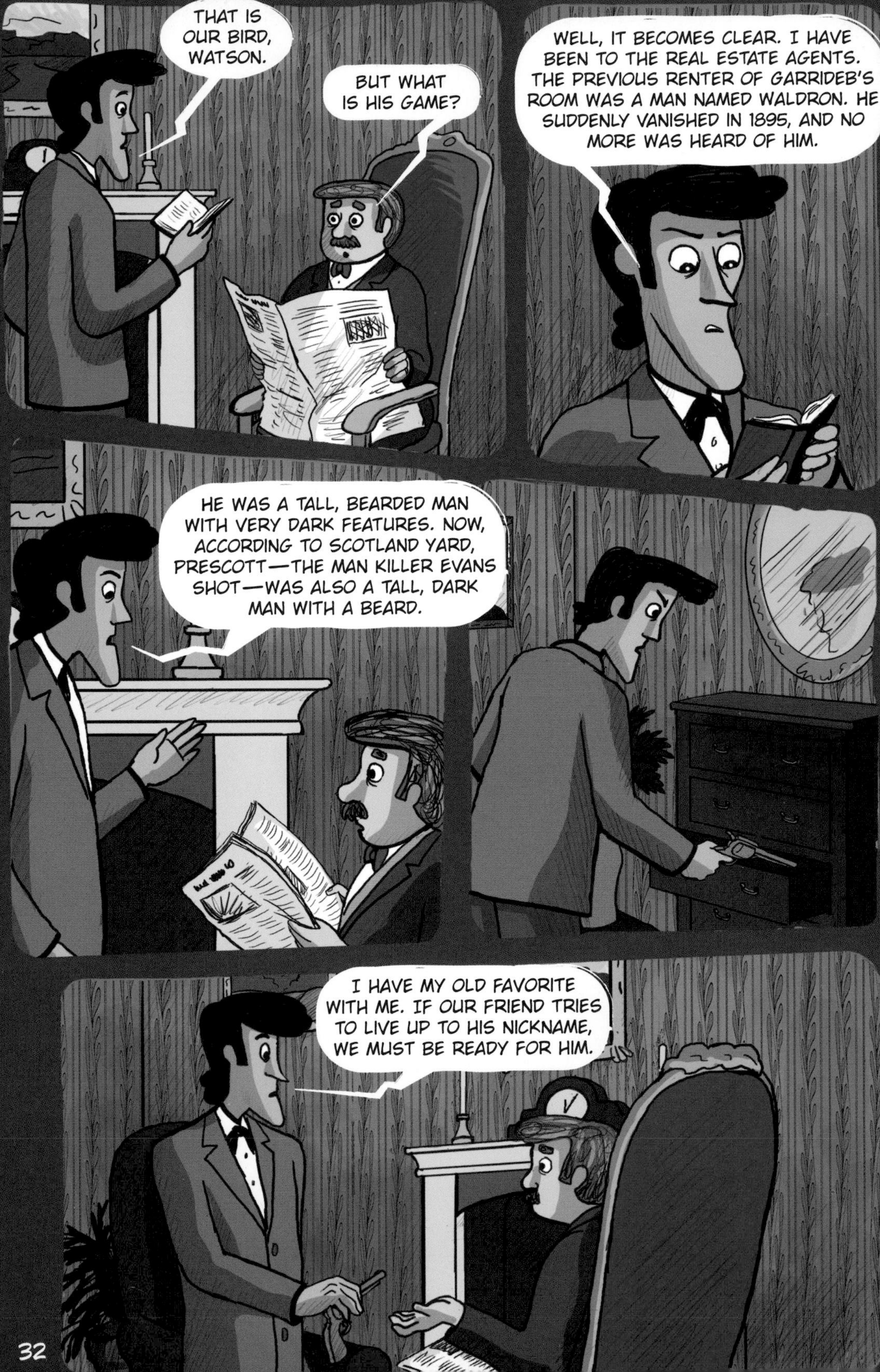
THAT IS OUR BIRD, WATSON.
BUT WHAT IS HIS GAME?
WELL, IT BECOMES CLEAR. I HAVE BEEN TO THE REAL ESTATE AGENTS. THE PREVIOUS RENTER OF GARRIDEB'S ROOM WAS A MAN NAMED WALDRON. HE SUDDENLY VANISHED IN 1895, AND NO MORE WAS HEARD OF HIM.
HE WAS A TALL, BEARDED MAN WITH VERY DARK FEATURES. NOW, ACCORDING TO SCOTLAND YARD, PRESCOTT—THE MAN KILLER EVANS SHOT—WAS ALSO A TALL, DARK MAN WITH A BEARD.
I HAVE MY OLD FAVORITE WITH ME. IF OUR FRIEND TRIES TO LIVE UP TO HIS NICKNAME, WE MUST BE READY FOR HIM.

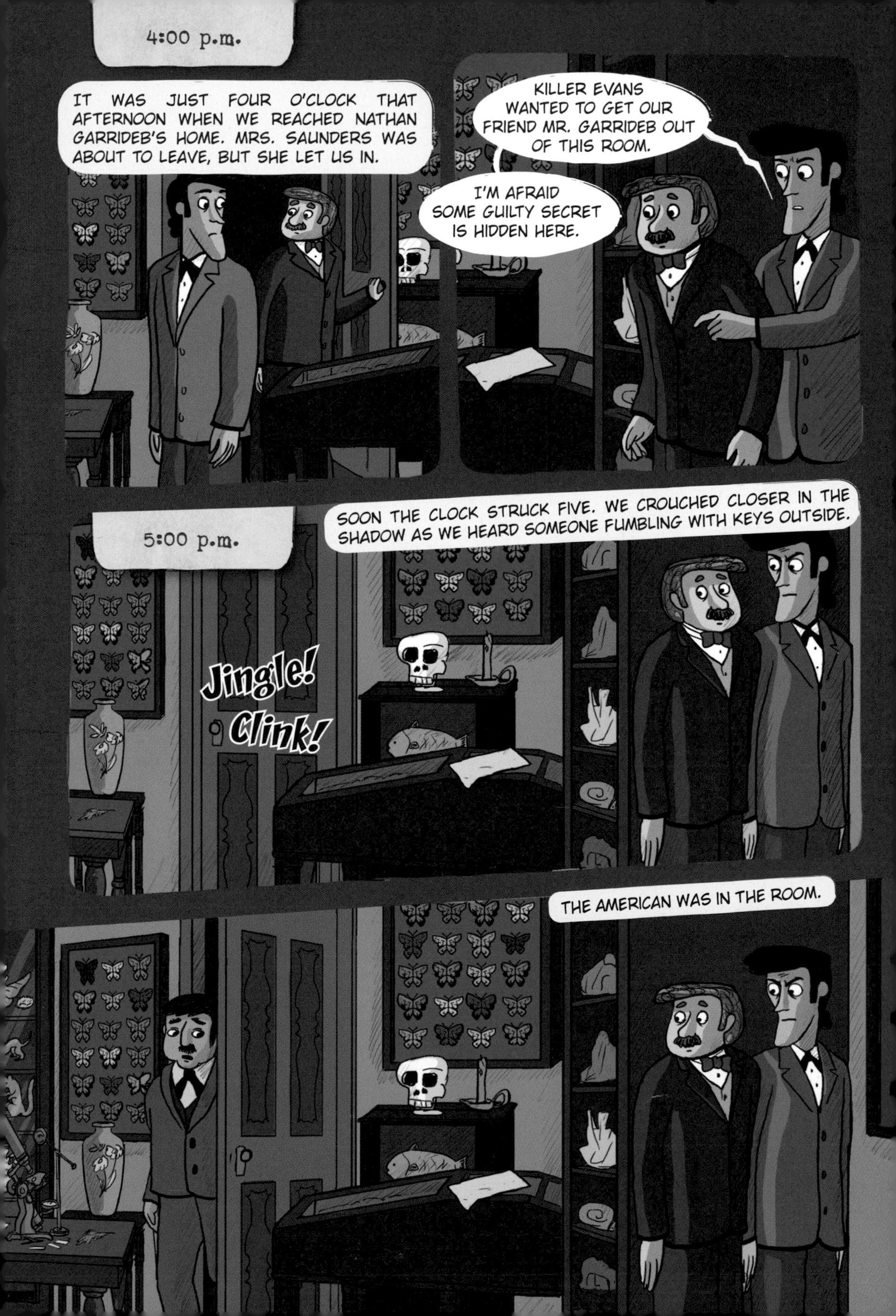
4:00 p.m.
IT WAS JUST FOUR O'CLOCK THAT AFTERNOON WHEN WE REACHED NATHAN GARRIDEB'S HOME. MRS. SAUNDERS WAS ABOUT TO LEAVE, BUT SHE LET US IN.
KILLER EVANS WANTED TO GET OUR FRIEND MR. GARRIDEB OUT OF THIS ROOM.
I'M AFRAID SOME GUILTY SECRET IS HIDDEN HERE.
5:00 p.m.
SOON THE CLOCK STRUCK FIVE. WE CROUCHED CLOSER IN THE SHADOW AS WE HEARD SOMEONE FUMBLING WITH KEYS OUTSIDE.
Jingle!
Clink!
THE AMERICAN WAS IN THE ROOM.

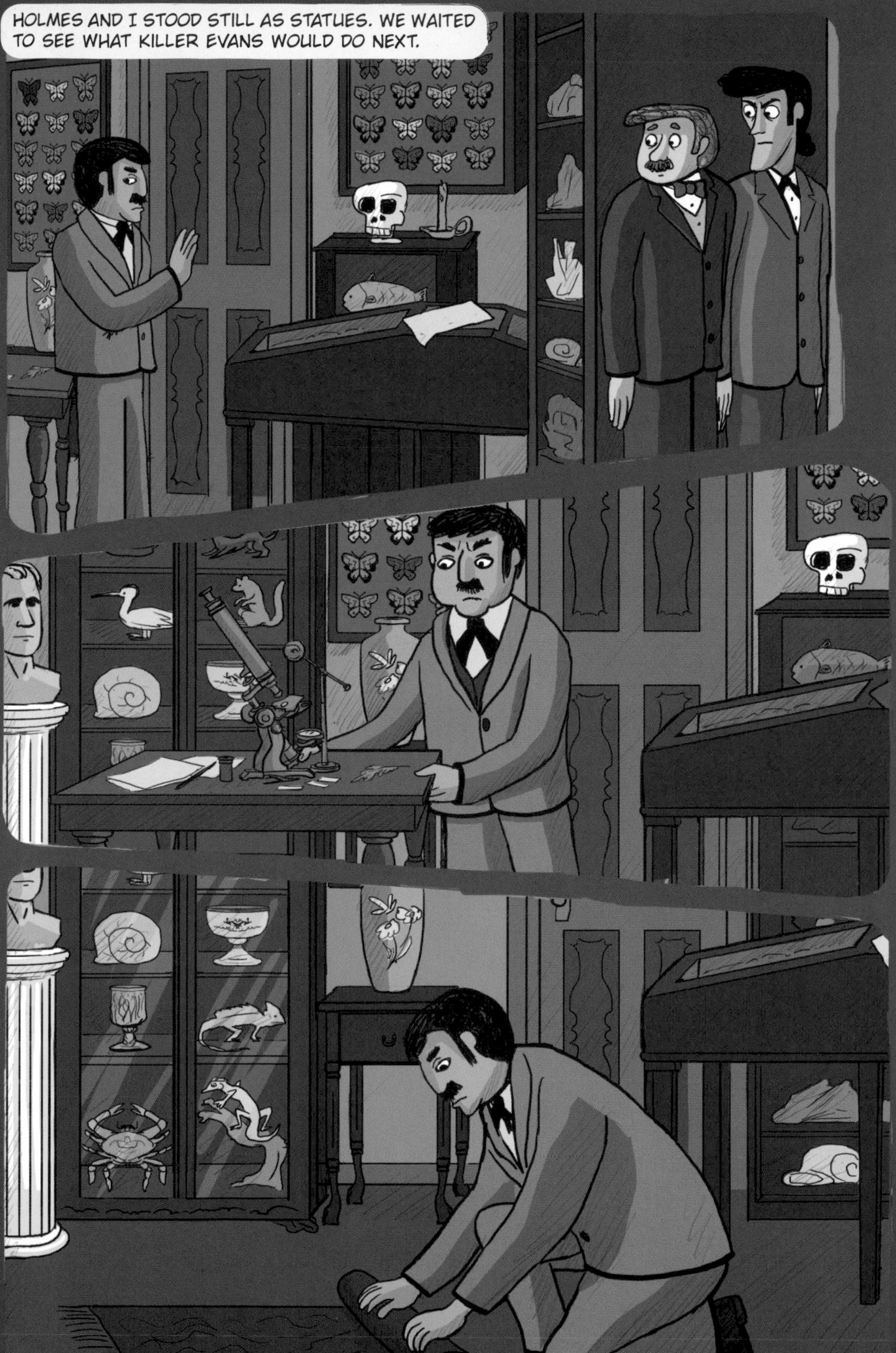
HOLMES AND I STOOD STILL AS STATUES. WE WAITED TO SEE WHAT KILLER EVANS WOULD DO NEXT.

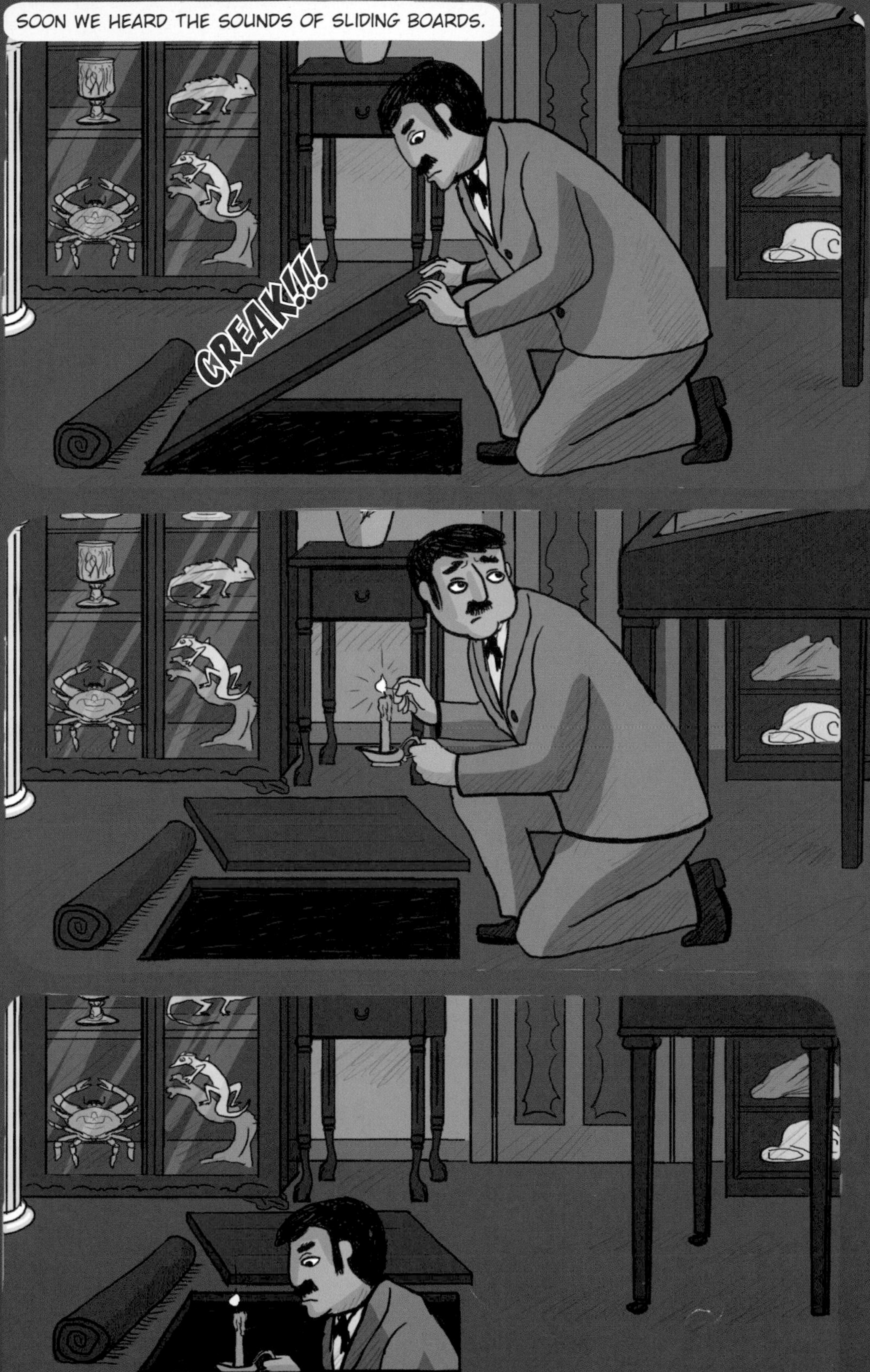
SOON WE HEARD THE SOUNDS OF SLIDING BOARDS.
CREAK!!!...

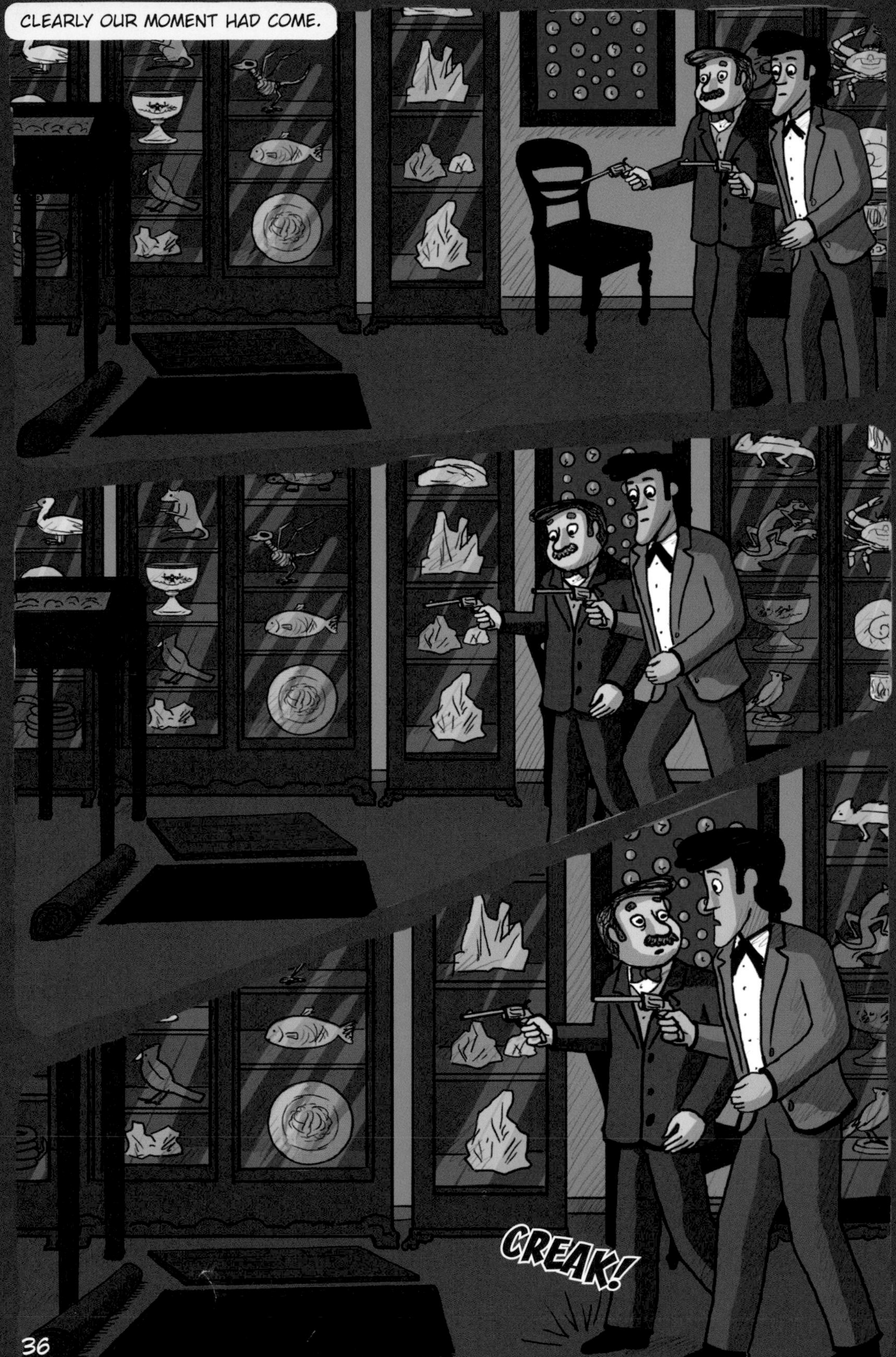

CLEARLY OUR MOMENT HAD COME.
CREAK!

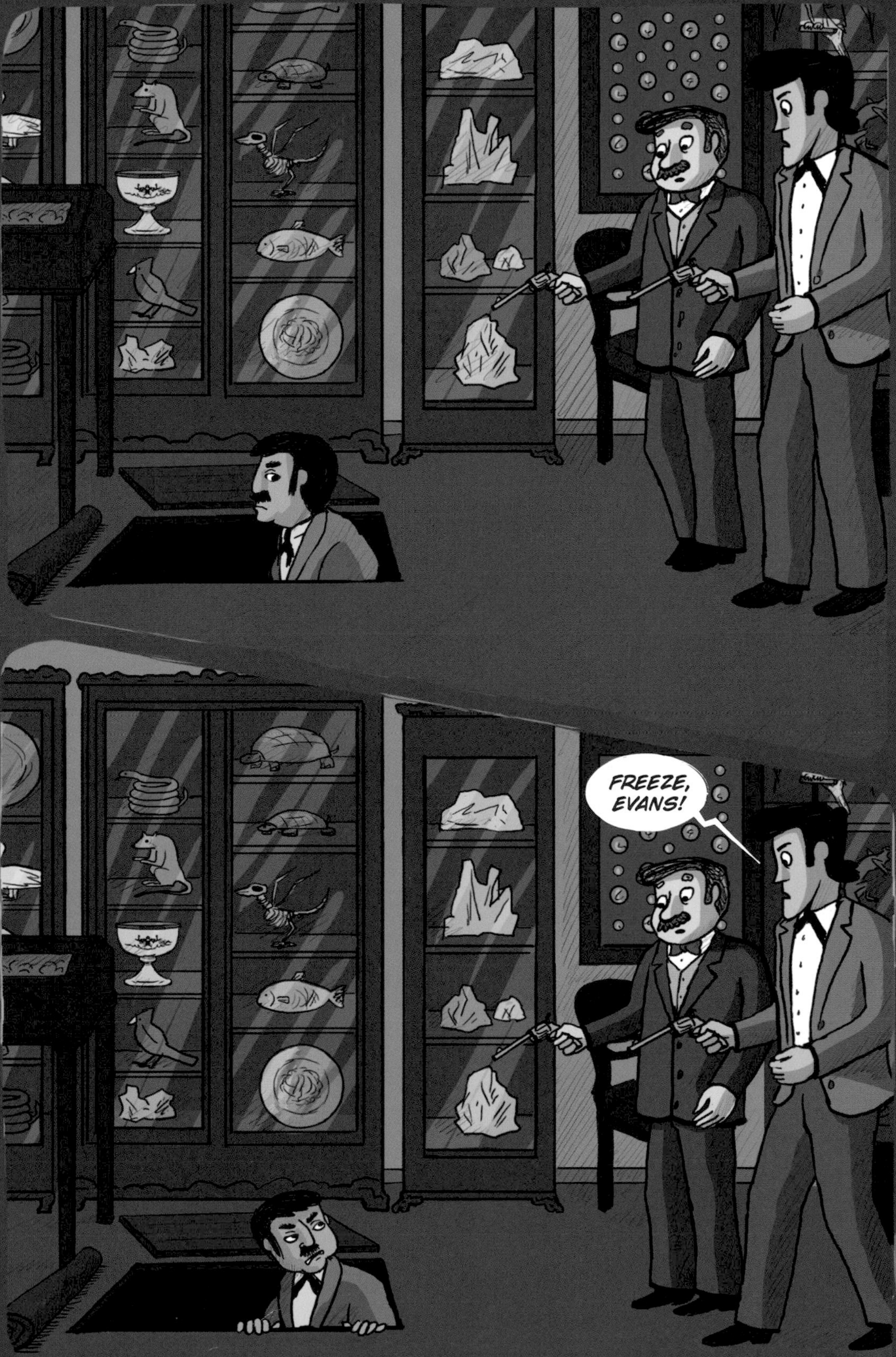
FREEZE, EVANS!

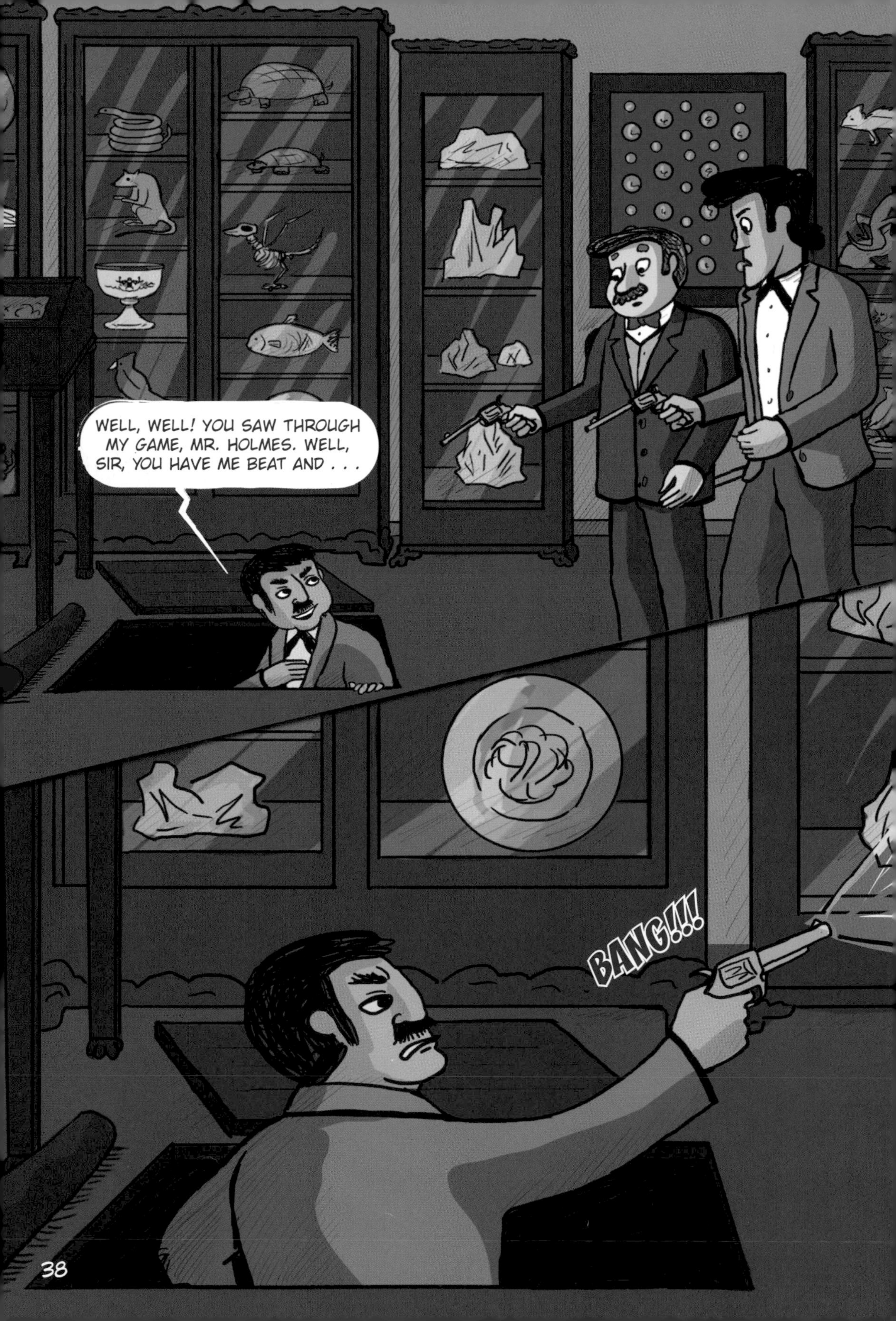
WELL, WELL! YOU SAW THROUGH MY GAME, MR. HOLMES. WELL, SIR, YOU HAVE ME BEAT AND . . .
BANG!!!

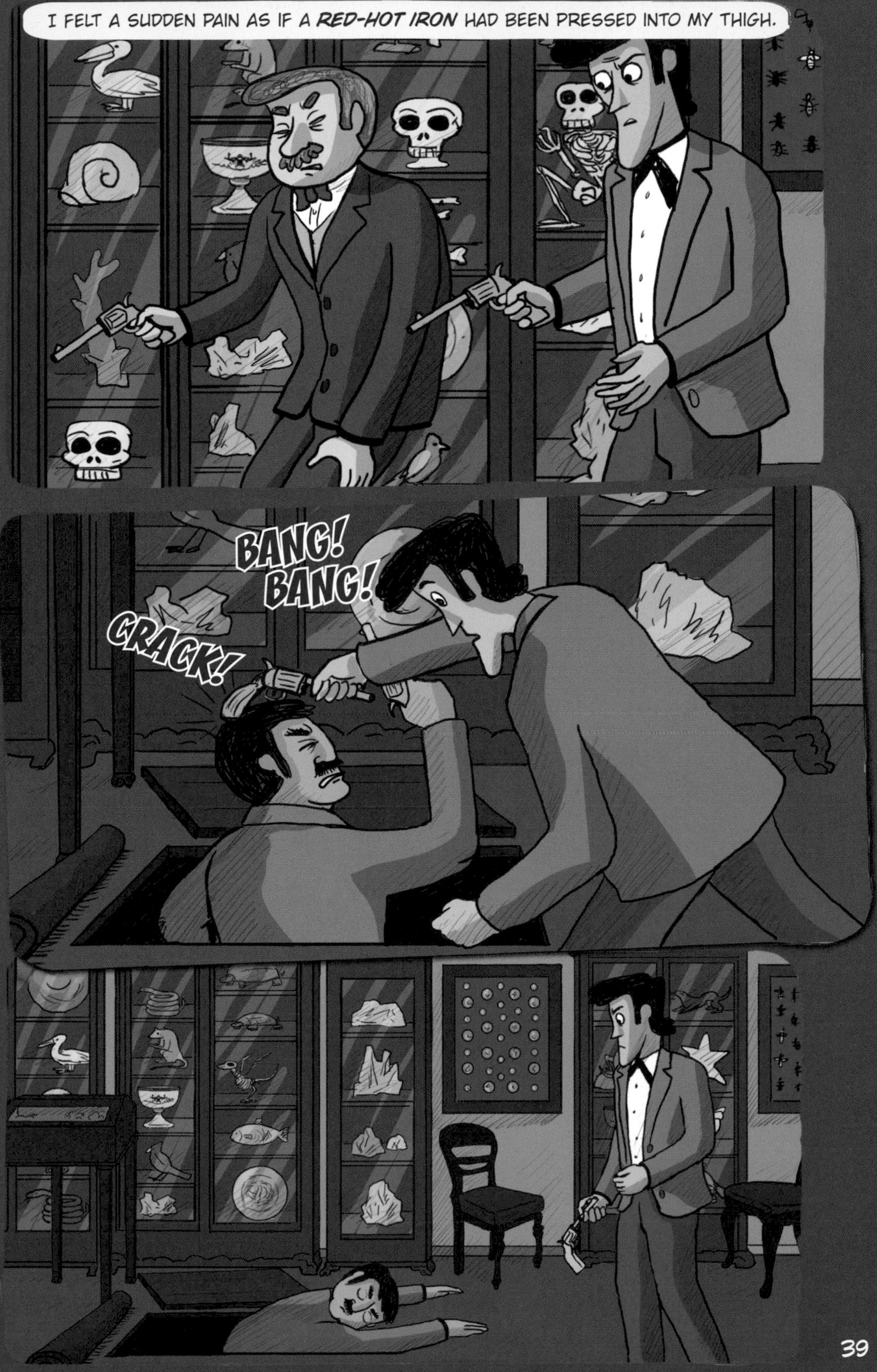
I FELT A SUDDEN PAIN AS IF A RED-HOT IRON HAD BEEN PRESSED INTO MY THIGH.
BANG!
BANG!
CRACK!

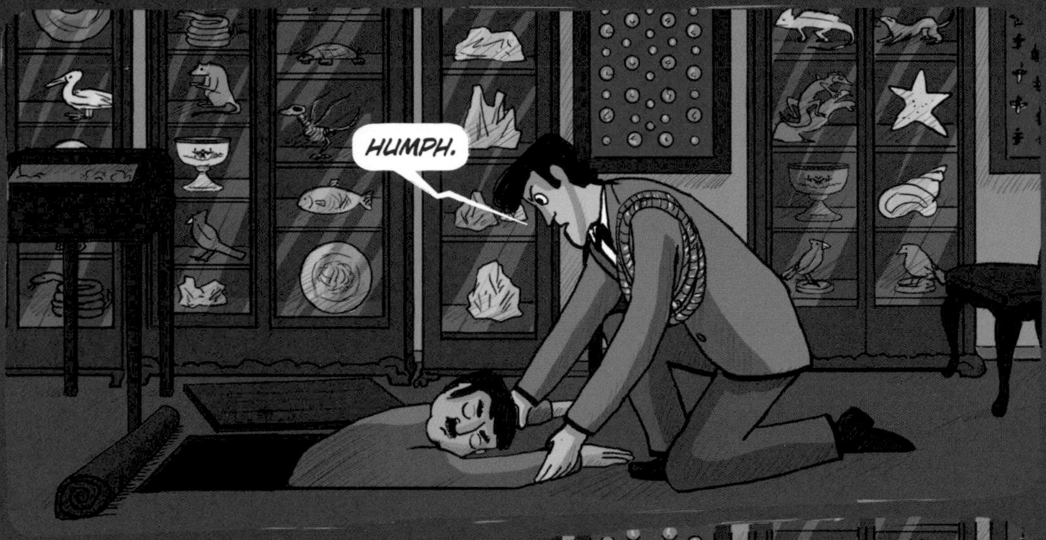
HUMPH.

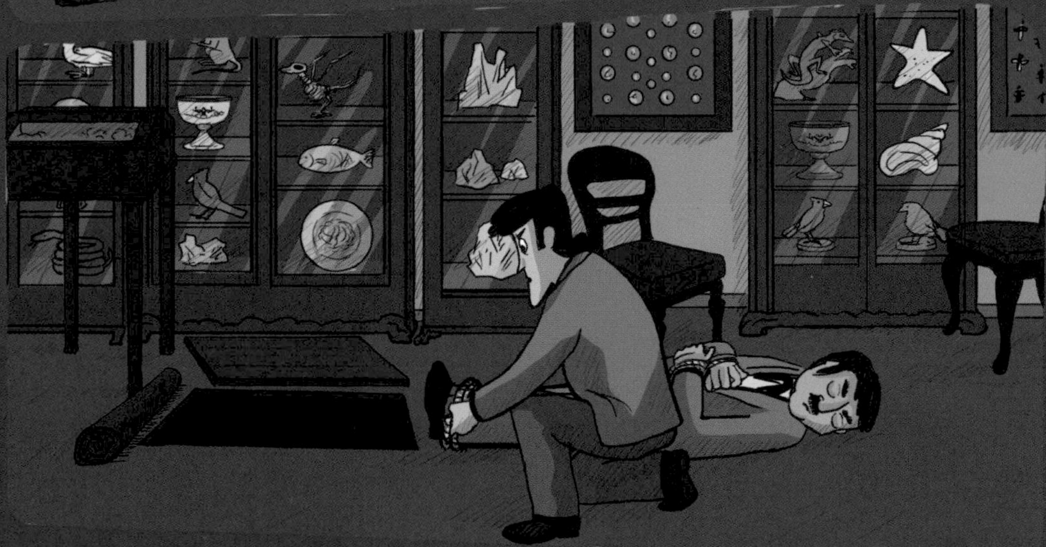

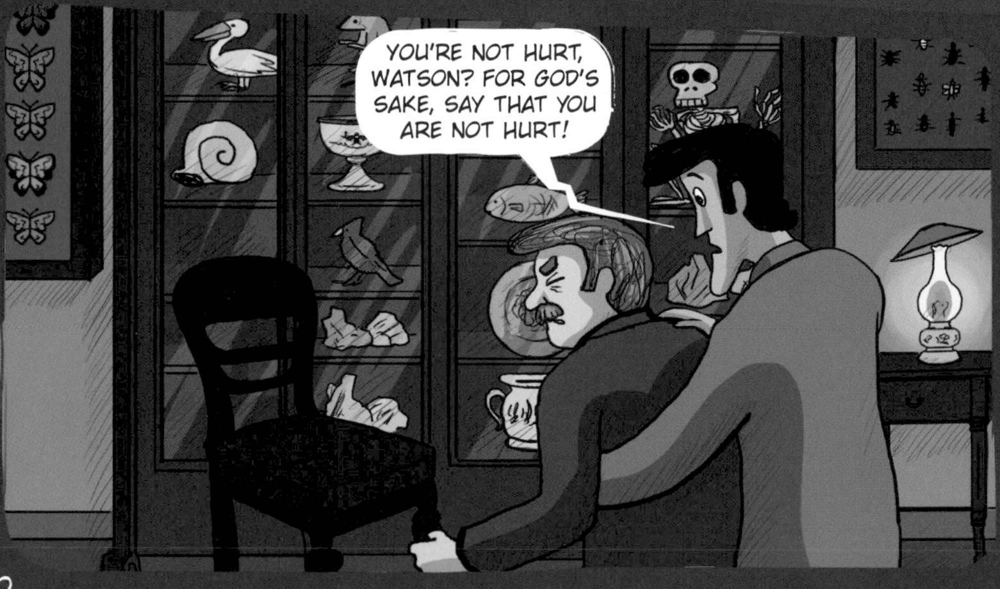
YOU'RE NOT HURT, WATSON? FOR GOD'S SAKE, SAY THAT YOU ARE NOT HURT!

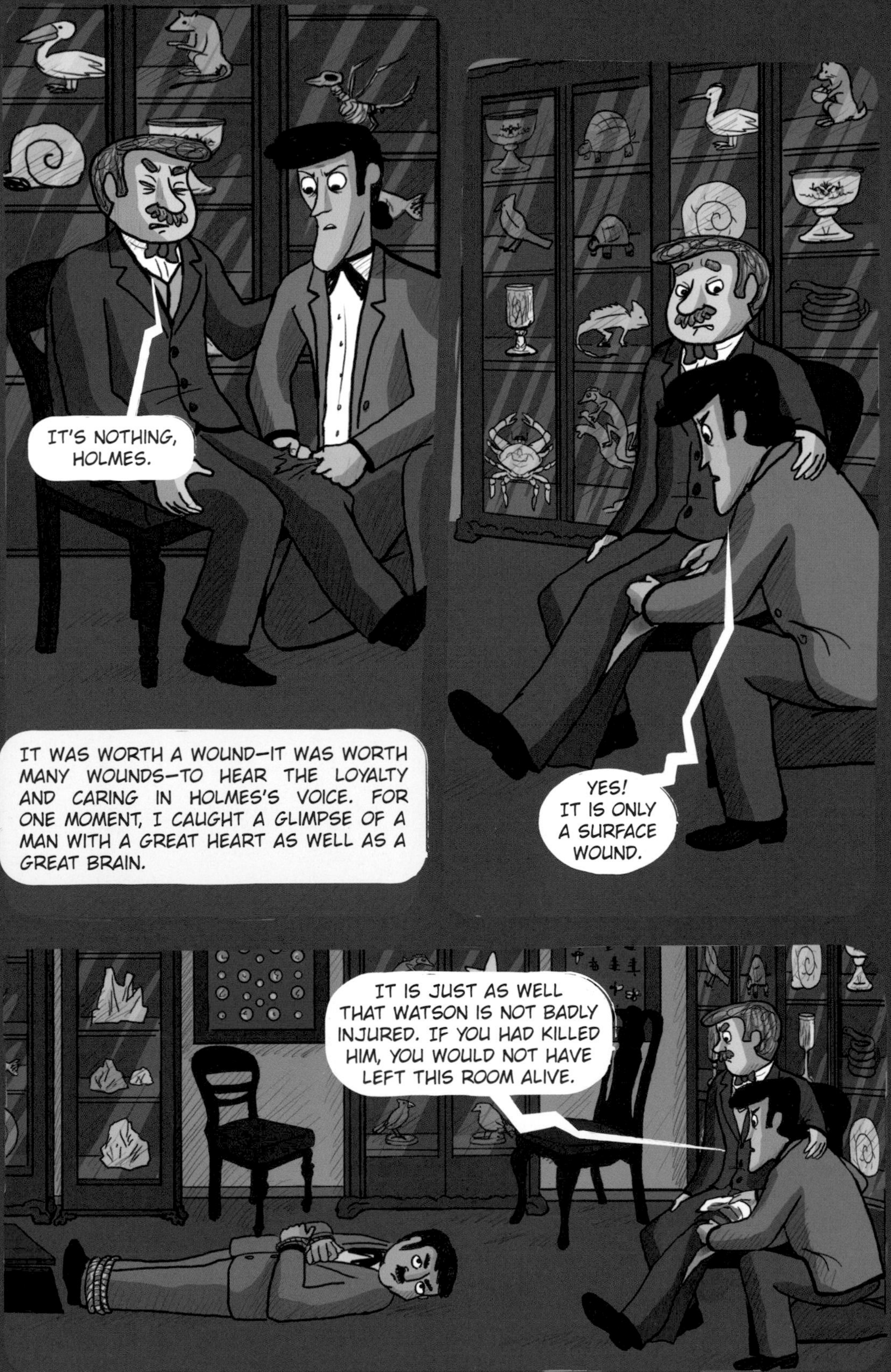
IT'S NOTHING, HOLMES.
IT WAS WORTH A WOUND—IT WAS WORTH MANY WOUNDS—TO HEAR THE LOYALTY AND CARING IN HOLMES'S VOICE. FOR ONE MOMENT, I CAUGHT A GLIMPSE OF A MAN WITH A GREAT HEART AS WELL AS A GREAT BRAIN.
YES! IT IS ONLY A SURFACE WOUND.
IT IS JUST AS WELL THAT WATSON IS NOT BADLY INJURED. IF YOU HAD KILLED HIM, YOU WOULD NOT HAVE LEFT THIS ROOM ALIVE.

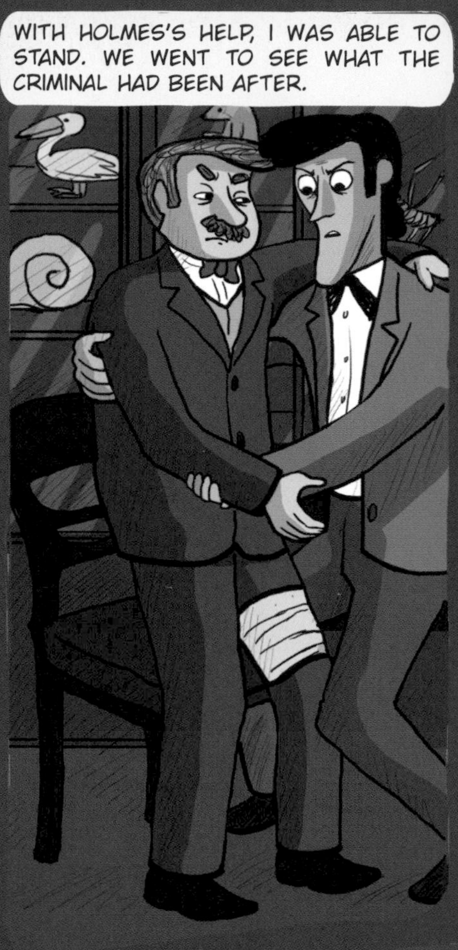
WITH HOLMES'S HELP, I WAS ABLE TO STAND. WE WENT TO SEE WHAT THE CRIMINAL HAD BEEN AFTER.

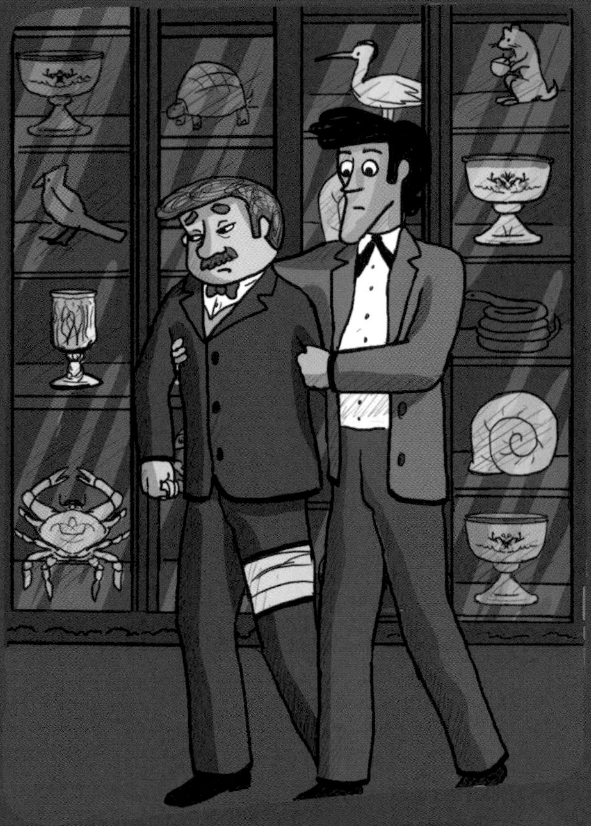

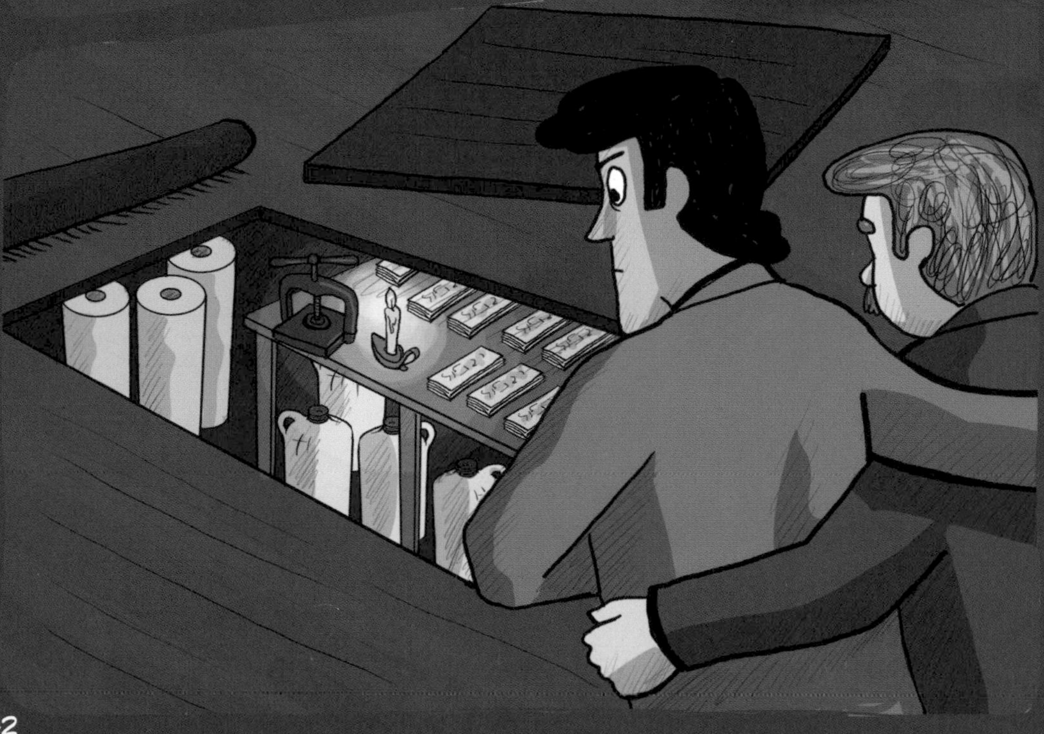

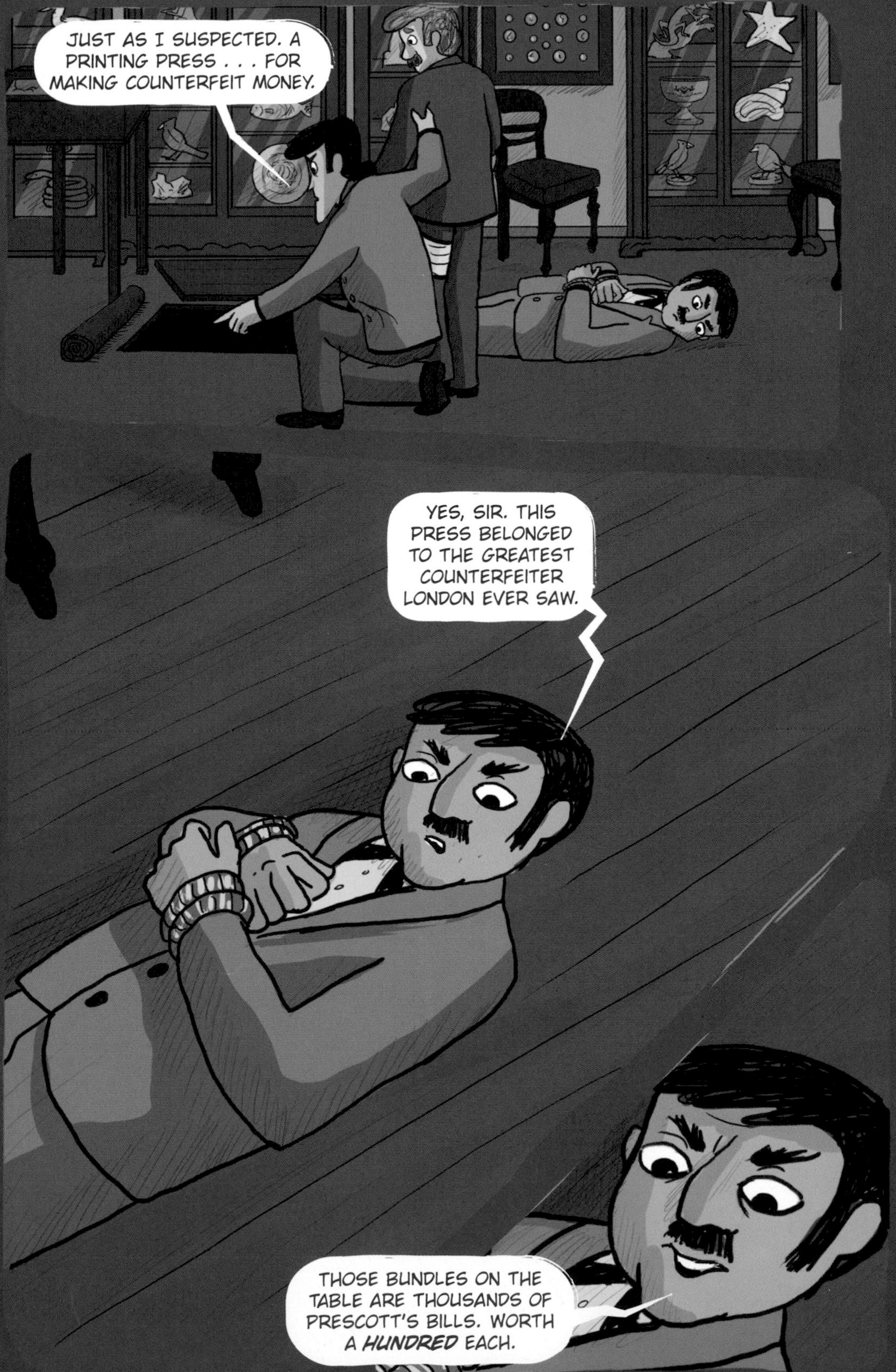
JUST AS I SUSPECTED. A PRINTING PRESS . . . FOR MAKING COUNTERFEIT MONEY.
YES, SIR. THIS PRESS BELONGED TO THE GREATEST COUNTERFEITER LONDON EVER SAW.
THOSE BUNDLES ON THE TABLE ARE THOUSANDS OF PRESCOTT'S BILLS. WORTH A *HUNDRED* EACH.

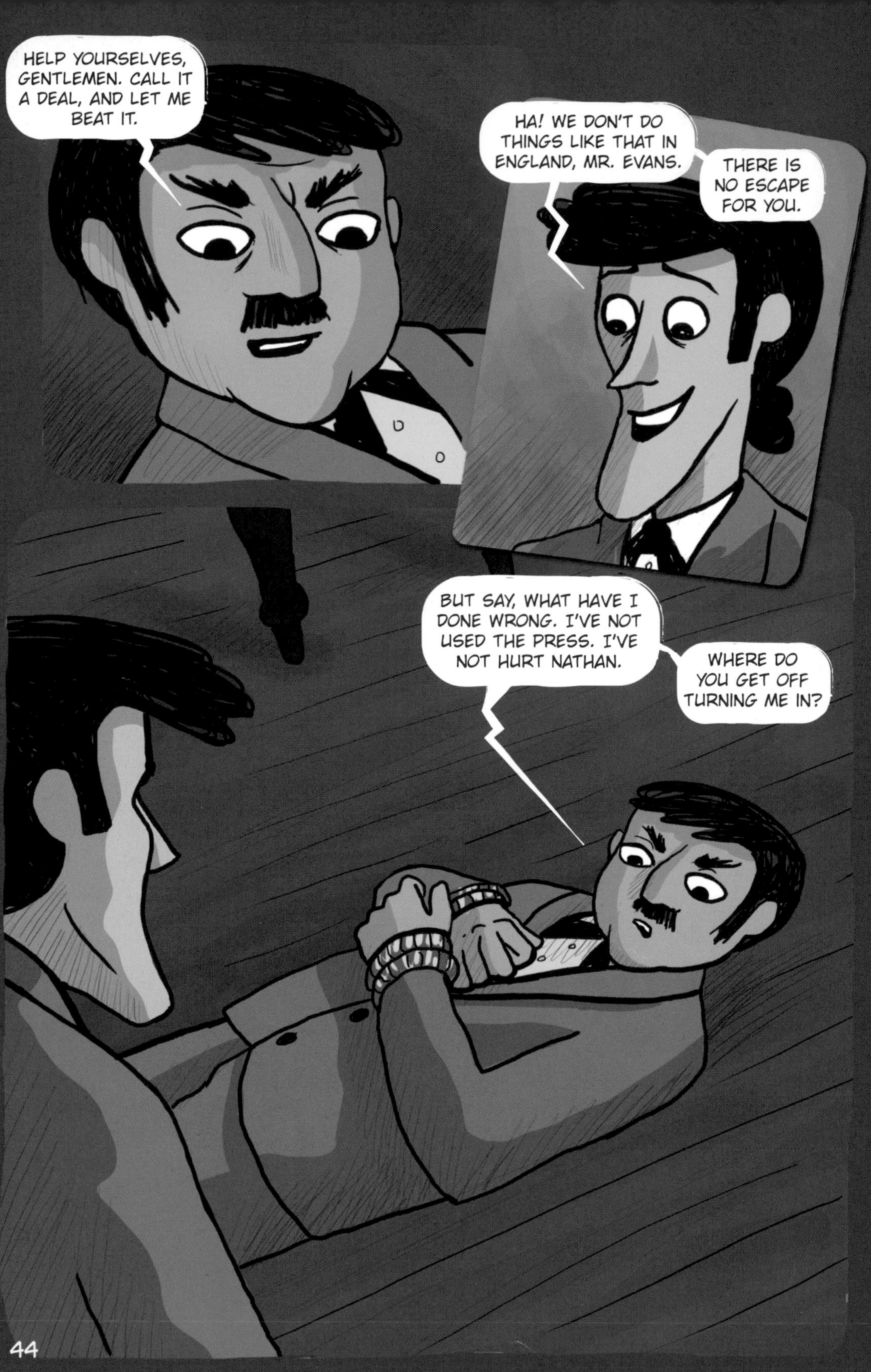
HELP YOURSELVES, GENTLEMEN. CALL IT A DEAL, AND LET ME BEAT IT.
HA! WE DON'T DO THINGS LIKE THAT IN ENGLAND, MR. EVANS.
THERE IS NO ESCAPE FOR YOU.
BUT SAY, WHAT HAVE I DONE WRONG. I'VE NOT USED THE PRESS. I'VE NOT HURT NATHAN.
WHERE DO YOU GET OFF TURNING ME IN?

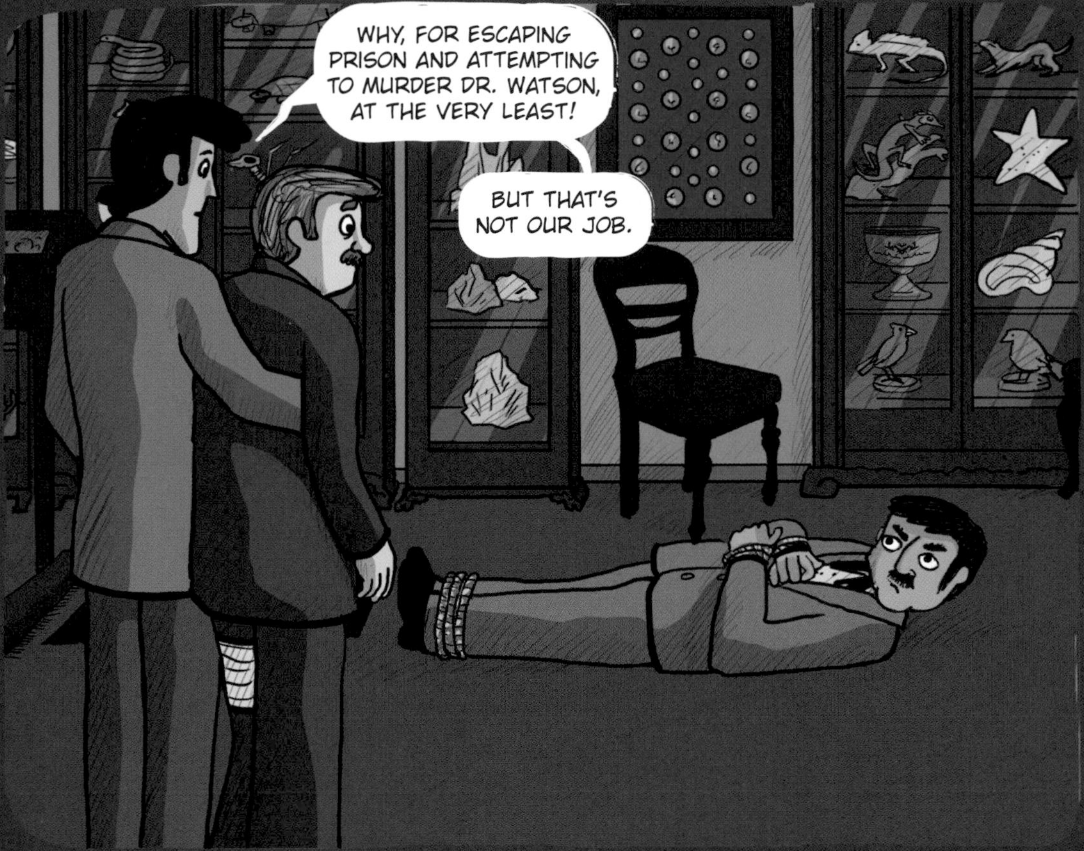
WHY, FOR ESCAPING PRISON AND ATTEMPTING TO MURDER DR. WATSON, AT THE VERY LEAST!
BUT THAT'S NOT OUR JOB.

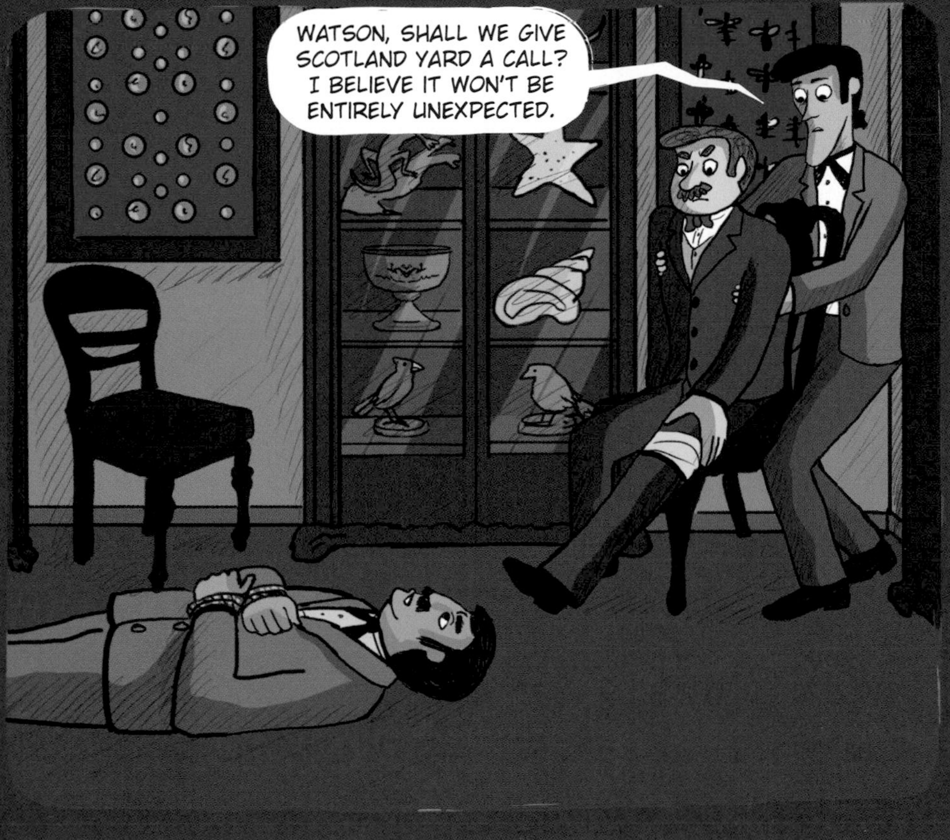
WATSON, SHALL WE GIVE SCOTLAND YARD A CALL? I BELIEVE IT WON'T BE ENTIRELY UNEXPECTED.

From the Desk of
John H. Watson, M.D.

The Adventure of the Three Garridebs: How Did Holmes Solve It?

What was it about John Garrideb that made Holmes suspicious?

John Garrideb claimed to have just arrived in England from America. Yet Holmes noticed that the style and cut of the man's clothes were definitely British. When Holmes suggested that the American had been in England for some time, John Garrideb was eager to change the subject.

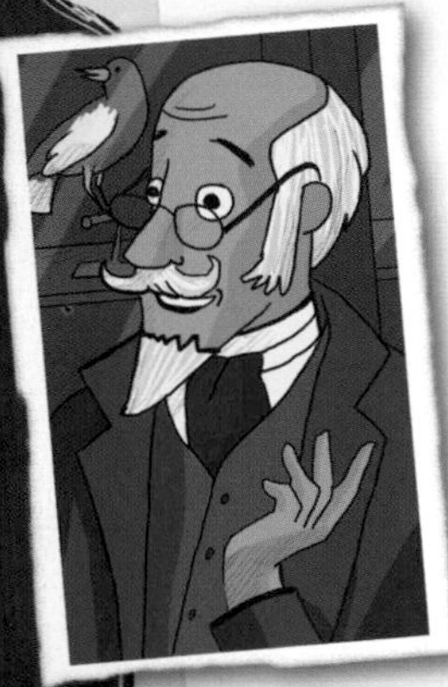

How was Holmes able to ascertain that John Garrideb was lying?

Holmes set a trap for the unsuspecting American when he made up his friend, Dr. Starr of Topeka, Kansas. When the man claimed to remember Starr, Holmes was certain that John Garrideb was not telling the truth. Holmes suspected the story of the three Garridebs was a lie as well, but he needed more clues to discover why the American had made up the strange tale.

How did Holmes know that Nathan Garrideb was innocent?

The brass nameplate at Nathan Garrideb's home had begun to discolor with age. Holmes concluded that Nathan Garrideb was not a fake, since his nameplate had been up for several years.

How did Holmes know that Nathan Garrideb's home held what the American wanted?

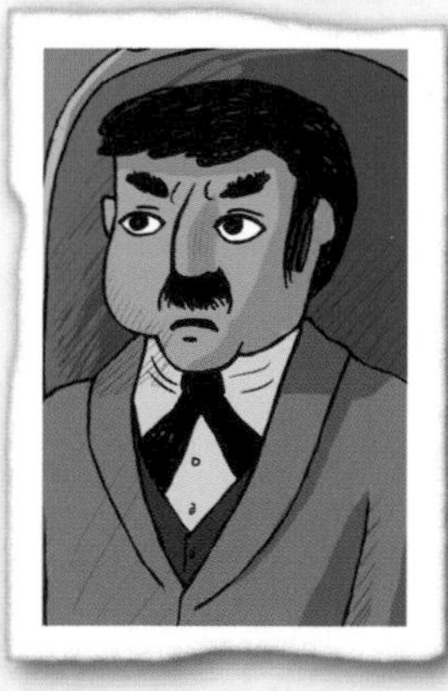

Holmes knew that Nathan Garrideb's trip to Birmingham was a wild-goose chase, because the advertisement was a fake. Since the older Garrideb never left his room, Holmes suspected that Garrideb's home must hold the key to the mystery. Nathan Garrideb had lived in his room since the previous tenant disappeared in 1895—the same year that a well-known counterfeiter, Roger Prescott, was murdered by the American criminal known as Killer Evans. Holmes guessed that Garrideb's room may once have been the headquarters of a counterfeit money operation.

Once Holmes learned John Garrideb's true identity, how was he able to piece together the mystery?

When Killer Evans, alias John Garrideb, headed straight for the trapdoor in the floor of Nathan Garrideb's home, Holmes's suspicions were confirmed. Roger Prescott must have shown the trapdoor to Killer Evans before he died. Holmes's discovery of the printing press and the thousands of fake bills solved the mystery of the three Garridebs.

Further Reading and Websites

Cosson, M. J. *The Mystery of the Too Crisp Cash.* Logan, IA: Perfection Learning, 1998.

Doyle, Sir Arthur Conan. *The Adventures and the Memoirs of Sherlock Holmes.* New York: Sterling, 2004.

Mason, Paul. *Frauds and Counterfeits.* Mankato, MN: Black Rabbit Books, 2010.

Shearer, Alex. *Canned.* New York: Scholastic, 2008.

Sherlock Holmes Museum
http://www.sherlock-holmes.co.uk

Sir Arthur Conan Doyle Society
http://www.ash-tree.bc.ca/acdsocy.html

Springer, Nancy. *The Case of the Bizarre Bouquets: An Enola Holmes Mystery.* New York: Penguin, 2009.

221 Baker Street
http://221bakerstreet.org

About the Author

Sir Arthur Conan Doyle was born on May 22, 1859. He became a doctor in 1882. When this career did not prove successful, Doyle started writing stories. In addition to the popular Sherlock Holmes short stories and novels, Doyle also wrote historical novels, romances, and plays.

About the Adapters

Murray Shaw's lifelong passion for Sherlock Holmes began when he was a child. He was the author of the Match Wits with Sherlock Holmes series published in the 1990s. For decades, he was a popular speaker in public schools and libraries on the adventures of Holmes and Watson.

M. J. Cosson is the author of more than fifty books, both fiction and nonfiction, for children and young adults. She has long been a fan of mysteries and especially of the great detective, Sherlock Holmes. In fact, she has participated in the production of several Sherlock Holmes plays. A native of Iowa, Cosson lives in the Texas Hill Country with her husband, dogs, and cat.

About the Illustrators

French artist Sophie Rohrbach began her career after graduating in display design at the Chambre des Commerce. She went on to design displays in many top department stores including Galerias Lafayette. She also studied illustration at Emile Cohl school in Lyon, France, where she now lives with her daughter. Rohrbach has illustrated many children's books. She is passionate about the colors and patterns that she uses in her illustrations.

JT Morrow has worked as a freelance illustrator for over twenty years and has won several awards. He specializes in doing parodies and imitations of the Old and Modern Masters—everyone from da Vinci to Picasso. JT also exhibits his paintings at galleries near his home. He lives just south of San Francisco with his wife and daughter.

DEADLY DISASTERS

Hurricanes, Typhoons, and Cyclones

Disaster & Survival

Bonnie J. Ceban

Enslow Publishers, Inc.

40 Industrial Road   PO Box 38
Box 398   Aldershot
Berkeley Heights, NJ 07922   Hants GU12 6BP
USA   UK
http://www.enslow.com

Library of Congress Cataloging-in-Publication Data:

Ceban, Bonnie J.
    Hurricanes, typhoons, and cyclones : disaster & survival / Bonnie J. Ceban.
        p. cm. — (Deadly disasters)
    Includes bibliographical references and index.
    ISBN-10: 0-7660-2388-5
    1. Storms—Juvenile literature. 2. Hurricanes—Juvenile literature.
    3. Typhoons—Juvenile literature. 4. Paleoclimatology—Juvenile literature.
    I. Title. II. Series.
    QC944.2.C38 2005
    551.55'2—dc22

                                                    2005007066

ISBN-13: 978-0-7660-2388-8

Printed in the United States of America

10 9 8 7 6 5 4 3 2

To Our Readers: We have done our best to make sure all Internet Addresses in this book were active and appropriate when we went to press. However, the author and the publisher have no control over and assume no liability for the material available on those Internet sites or on other Web sites they may link to. Any comments or suggestions can be sent by e-mail to comments@enslow.com or to the address on the back cover.

Illustration Credits: Associated Press, AP, pp. 4, 7, 23, 25, 27, 28, 39; Associated Press, KYODO NEWS, pp. 32, 33; Associated Press, ST. PETERSBURG TIMES, pp. 1, 6; Associated Press, UN/MINUSTAH, p. 8; Associated Press, NISHINIPPON SHIMBUN, p. 31; Associated Press, NOAA/NATIONAL HURRICANE CENTER, p. 11 (bottom); Enslow Publishers, Inc., pp. 11 (top), 18; National Hurricane Center, p. 13; National Library of Australia, courtesy of R. Keirison, p. 20; National Library of Australia, photo by Barry Le Lievre, p. 19; NOAA, p. 35; Photos.com, p. 37.

Cover Illustration: Associated Press, ST. PETERSBURG TIMES

Contents

The force of Hurricane Charley caved in the roofs of many houses in its path.

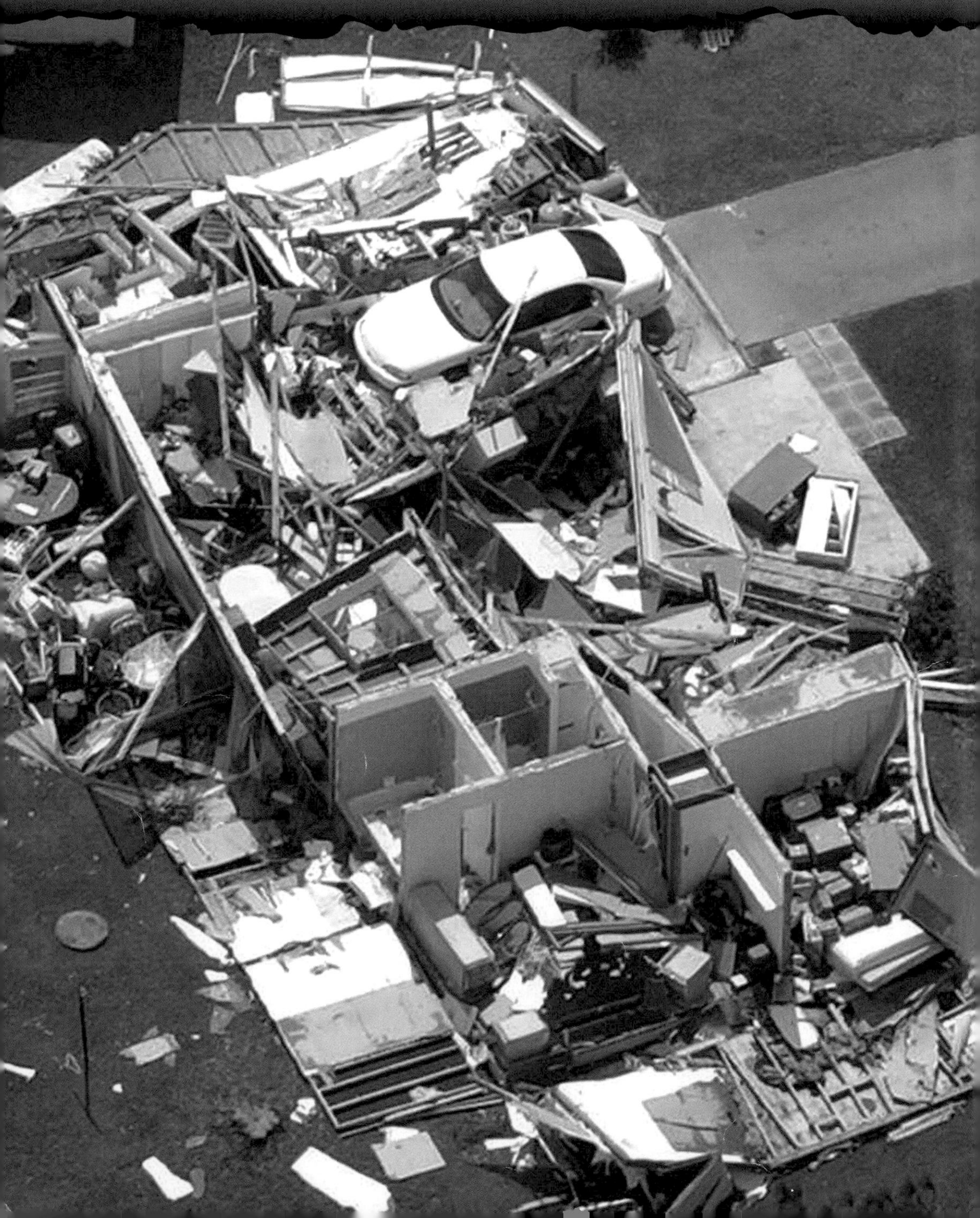

1

A Record-Breaking Season

HURRICANE SEASON 2004 ROARED THROUGH FLORIDA. For the first time in history, four massive storms hit the state in one season. Billions of dollars in damages were caused by the four-hit power punch.

One After the Other

Hurricane Charley came through Florida in the middle of August, leaving $20 billion in damage. Thousands of people were instantly homeless. Thirteen people died.[1]

Hurricane Frances barreled through two weeks after Charley. Frances caused heavy rains, including over eighteen inches in Linville Falls, North Carolina.[2] The storm killed five people in Florida.[3] Next came Hurricane Ivan. This storm killed ninety-two people over its entire path, including twenty-five in the United States.[4]

5

Indian River Drive in Jensen Beach, Florida, was washed out due to flooding from Hurricane Frances.

Hurricane Jeanne arrived at the end of September. It raged across Florida with 120 mile-per-hour winds.[5] It caused major flooding and killed four people.[6]

Tumbling Roofs

The Turner Agri-Civic Center was a Red Cross shelter that was built to withstand hurricane-force winds. Therefore, the fourteen hundred people there were confident that they would be protected from Hurricane Charley.

However, as the storm intensified, the building began to collapse. As the roof on the Turner Agri-Civic Center came falling down, Freddie Lou Gladstone was right in the center of it all. "The roof didn't just blow off—it went crack, crack, piece by piece like a house tumbling down," said Gladstone. "Young girls, thirteen or fourteen years old, were grabbing each other and just screaming."[7] Luckily, no one was killed in the collapse.

A worker rests and drinks some water on the roof of Charlotte Medical Center. The hospital was damaged when Charley blew through.

The Turner Center was not the only building to lose a roof that night. The Charlotte Medical Center also lost its roof. Many patients were transported to other facilities until repairs could be made.

An Island Suffers

Tropical storm Jeanne hit Haiti prior to slamming into Florida as a hurricane. The floods it caused in Haiti killed more than three thousand people and fully destroyed over four thousand homes.[8]

Tropical storm Jeanne caused mass flooding throughout Haiti. Many people lost their lives to the turbulent waters.

Medira Jarmis fled Gonaives where the storm had done major damage. "There are so many deaths that the place stinks, and there is nothing to eat or drink."[9]

Even aid workers were overwhelmed: "The hygiene situation is appalling. There is no running water, no latrine [bathroom]," said Maita Alvarez.[10]

There were hundreds of millions of dollars in damages. In order to prevent such widespread damage in the future, scientists are studying hurricanes, typhoons, and cyclones to learn how to best prepare for them.

CHAPTER

2

The Science of Hurricanes, Typhoons, and Cyclones

WHAT IS THE DIFFERENCE BETWEEN A HURRICANE, a typhoon, and a cyclone? They are actually the same storm, what meteorologists (weather scientists) call tropical cyclones.[1] However, in different parts of the world, they are called different names. Hurricanes form in the Atlantic Ocean and eastern Pacific Ocean regions. These storms follow paths that mainly affect the Caribbean Islands, Mexico, the United States, and South America. Typhoons form over the tropical regions of the western Pacific Ocean. Their paths affect Japan, China, Indonesia, and other countries in Southeast Asia.

Finally, cyclones form over the Bay of Bengal, the Indian Ocean, and the South China Sea. These storms will affect Australia, South Asia, and the southeast coast of Africa.[2]

Hurricanes, typhoons, and cyclones are all intense, low-pressure, rapidly rotating storm systems.[3] These storms can be as wide as one thousand miles. The sustained winds can reach over 180 miles per hour. The gusts of wind can reach over 200 miles per hour. Tropical cyclones can also cause storm surges. These cause the ocean's tides to be higher than normal. These powerful storm surges, along with the pouring rains, can create massive flood damage.[4]

Formation: Where and When?

Tropical cyclones generally form in the tropics.[5] This is the area on a globe between the Tropic of Cancer and the Tropic of Capricorn.

Although a tropical cyclone can move onto land, it always forms over the sea and gains power over water. Once a tropical cyclone reaches land, its winds die down within a day or two.

A tropical cyclone has a circular shape. In the center is a small area with no wind, called "the eye." Around the eye, masses of storm clouds called the "eye wall" rotate. Some stormy areas stretch out from the eye wall and are

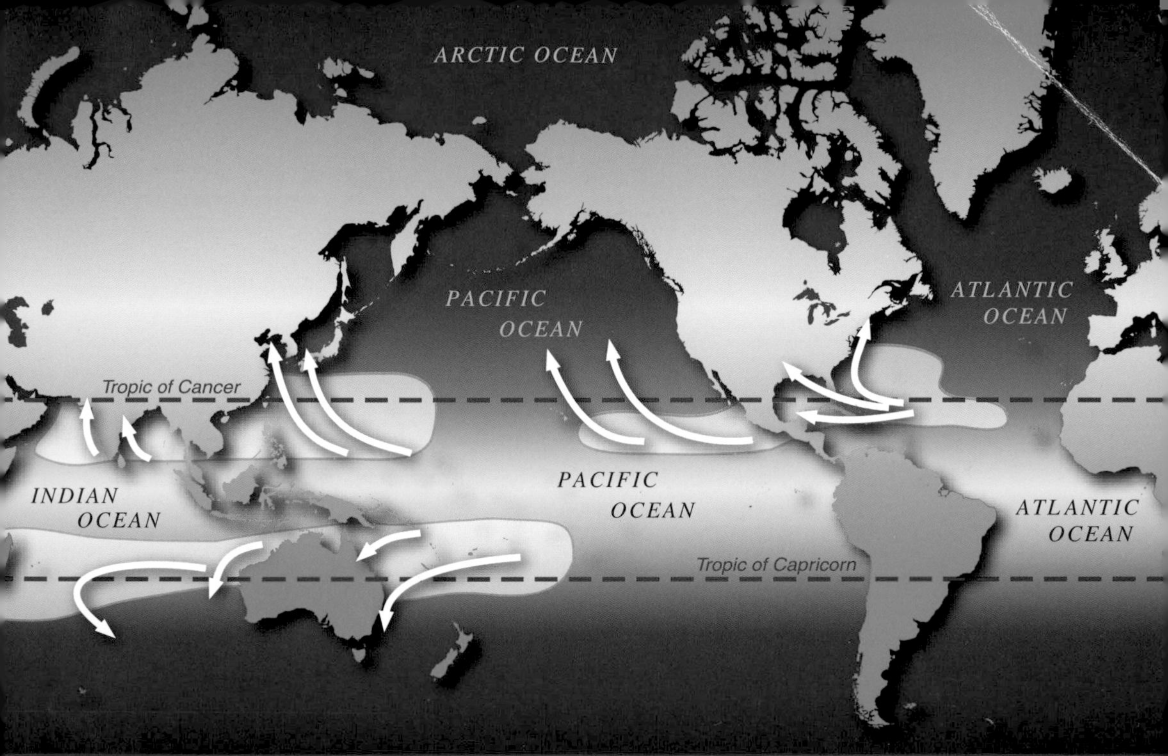
ARCTIC OCEAN
PACIFIC OCEAN
ATLANTIC OCEAN
Tropic of Cancer
INDIAN OCEAN
PACIFIC OCEAN
ATLANTIC OCEAN
Tropic of Capricorn

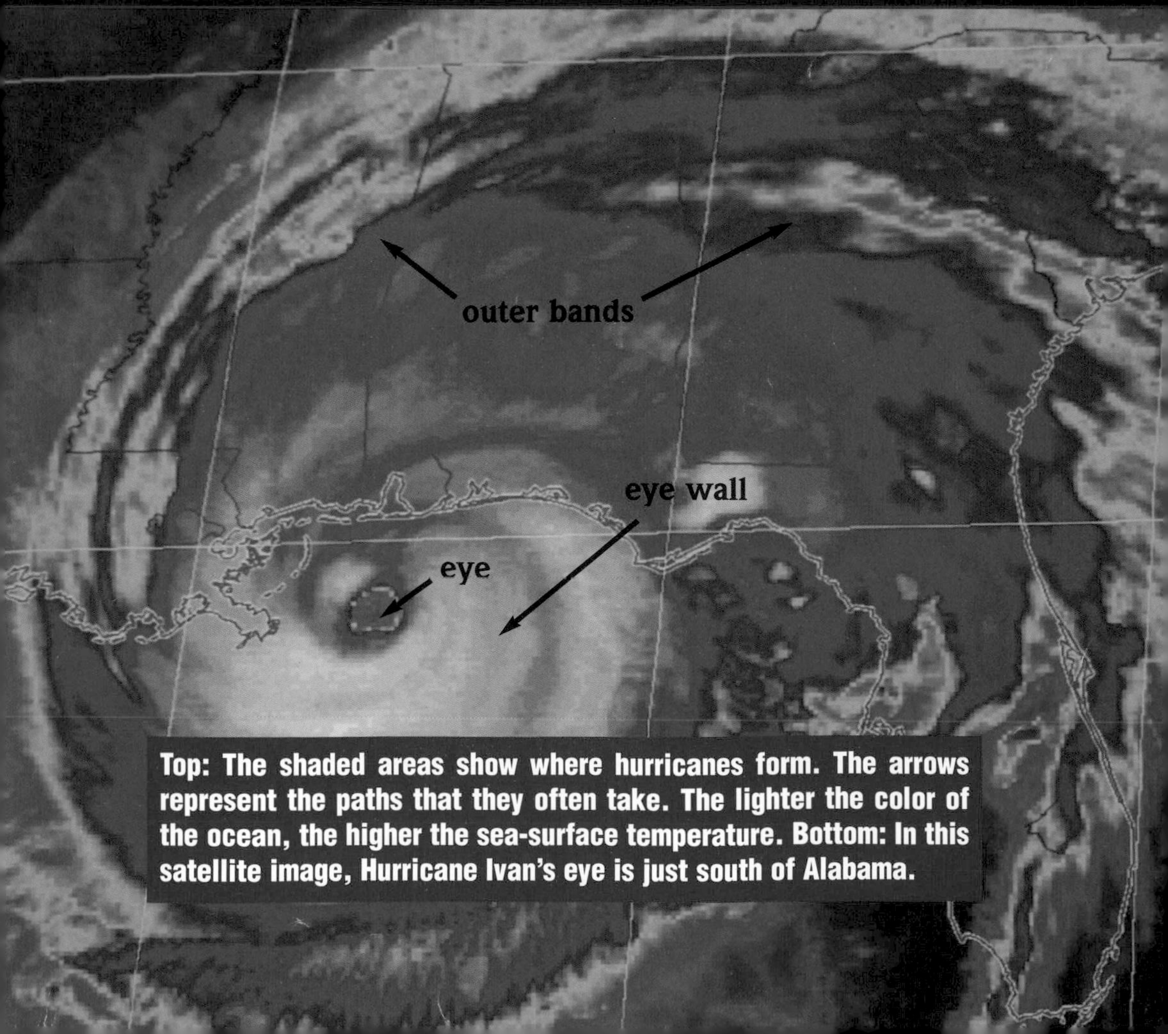
outer bands
eye wall
eye

Top: The shaded areas show where hurricanes form. The arrows represent the paths that they often take. The lighter the color of the ocean, the higher the sea-surface temperature. Bottom: In this satellite image, Hurricane Ivan's eye is just south of Alabama.

called "outer bands." Even after the eye wall has passed, the outer bands may still affect an area and cause heavy rain, thunderstorms, and even tornadoes.[6]

Most tropical cyclones form in the summer and fall. In the United States, June 1 to November 30 is called "hurricane season." During this time, the sea-surface temperature is high enough to allow for storm formation.[7]

Formation: How?

Tropical cyclones generally form gradually, over a series of days. First, a tropical wave will form. This is not an actual ocean wave, but a stormy area of low atmospheric pressure. Next, a tropical depression will form from the tropical wave. A tropical depression has winds of up to 31 miles per hour. If the tropical depression passes over a warm area of sea, a tropical depression can then evolve into a tropical storm with winds from 32 to 73 miles per hour. A tropical storm has gained enough power to become classified as a tropical cyclone once its winds are 74 miles per hour or more.

Meteorologists can predict that a tropical cyclone may form. One clue is a cluster of thunderstorms over the ocean. If the surface temperature of the sea is higher than 80° Fahrenheit, then the storm may become more severe. A drop in atmospheric pressure also may indicate that the storm will worsen.

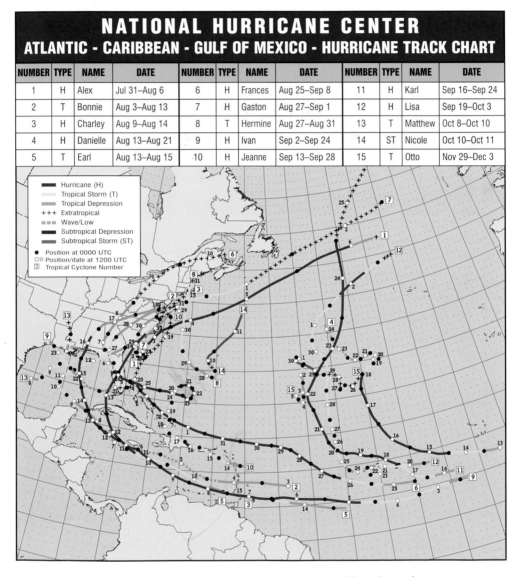

NATIONAL HURRICANE CENTER
ATLANTIC - CARIBBEAN - GULF OF MEXICO - HURRICANE TRACK CHART

NUMBER	TYPE	NAME	DATE	NUMBER	TYPE	NAME	DATE	NUMBER	TYPE	NAME	DATE
1	H	Alex	Jul 31–Aug 6	6	H	Frances	Aug 25–Sep 8	11	H	Karl	Sep 16–Sep 24
2	T	Bonnie	Aug 3–Aug 13	7	H	Gaston	Aug 27–Sep 1	12	H	Lisa	Sep 19–Oct 3
3	H	Charley	Aug 9–Aug 14	8	T	Hermine	Aug 27–Aug 31	13	T	Matthew	Oct 8–Oct 10
4	H	Danielle	Aug 13–Aug 21	9	H	Ivan	Sep 2–Sep 24	14	ST	Nicole	Oct 10–Oct 11
5	T	Earl	Aug 13–Aug 15	10	H	Jeanne	Sep 13–Sep 28	15	T	Otto	Nov 29–Dec 3

Hurricane (H)
Tropical Storm (T)
Tropical Depression
+++ Extratropical
Wave/Low
Subtropical Depression
Subtropical Storm (ST)
Position at 0000 UTC
Position/date at 1200 UTC
Tropical Cyclone Number

The year 2004 was a busy hurricane season. The chart shows all the hurricane tracks for that year. Notice how all the hurricanes begin as tropical depressions.

The Coriolis effect is also an important factor in the formation of these storms. It was identified by French physicist Gustave-Gaspard de Coriolis in 1835. It means that when the earth rotates, it causes winds, ocean currents, and other moving objects to be deflected from their original path. This, then, causes rotation of air around both low- and high-pressure systems.[8]

A tropical depression is a low pressure system. When it forms, the Coriolis effect causes air to rotate around it. In the Northern Hemisphere of the world, the storm rotates clockwise. In the Southern Hemisphere, the storm rotates counterclockwise.[9]

Hurricane Names

Each hurricane is assigned a name. The World Meteorological Organization assigns the Atlantic six lists of names. One list is used each year. After the sixth year, the list rotation goes back to the first one.[10]

On each list, every name starts with a different letter. The first hurricane of the season starts with the letter "A," then "B," and so forth. However, the letters "Q," "U," "X," "Y," and "Z" are not used.[11] The names on the list alternate between boys' and girls' names. When an unusually strong storm hits, its name is taken off the list. It is then replaced with a name with the same starting letter as the name that was removed.

Damage Scale

The National Weather Service uses a simple damage scale (shown below) to assess the power of a hurricane. It is called the Saffir-Simpson Scale.

Whether Category 1 or Category 5, hurricanes, along with cyclones and typhoons, are very dangerous storms. Survivors always have a story to tell.

Saffir-Simpson Scale

Category	Sustained Winds	Damage	Example Storms
1	74–95 mph	Minimal: Damage to plants and trees, and unanchored mobile homes. No real structural damage.	Hurricane Irene, 1999
2	96–110	Moderate: Some trees blown down. Major damage to exposed mobile homes. Some damage to roofs, windows, and doors.	Hurricane Floyd, 1999 Hurricane Frances, 2004
3	111–130	Extensive: Large trees blown down. Mobile homes destroyed. Some damage to roofs of buildings. Some structural damage to small buildings.	Hurricane Fran, 1996 Hurricane Ivan, 2004
4	131–155	Extreme: Large trees blown down. Complete destruction of mobile homes. Extensive damage to roofs, windows, and doors. Roofs destroyed on many small homes.	Hurricane Hugo, 1989 Hurricane Charley, 2004
5	>155	Catastrophic: Roofs destroyed on many homes and industrial buildings. Extensive damage to windows and doors. Some buildings completely destroyed.[12]	Hurricane Camille, 1969 Hurricane Andrew, 1992

A Tragic Christmas Day

I T WAS A CALM AND JOYFUL CHRISTMAS SEASON IN the city of Darwin, Australia. However, a severe storm that seemed at a harmless distance was about to change its path. Cyclone Tracy would create one of the worst tragedies in Australian history.

An Unprepared City

Darwin was home to approximately forty-eight thousand people in December 1974. However, the government report on Cyclone Tracy states, "This population was housed in approximately 12,000 dwellings. Unhappily, few residents realized that most of these dwellings would have little or no capacity to withstand cyclonic forces."[1]

The Cyclone

On December 20, 1974, the Australian Bureau of Meteorology monitored a tropical depression forming 435 miles northeast of Darwin in the Arafura Sea. By December 21, winds intensified and the depression was upgraded to cyclone status. Once upgraded, the bureau gave it the next name in the registry: Tracy.[2]

On December 22, ABC News Radio reported: "Cyclone Tracy poses no immediate threat to Darwin."[3] Cyclone Tracy soon passed the western tip of Bathurst Island, well north of Darwin. However, in the early morning hours of December 24, Tracy changed direction and sped toward the unprepared city.[4]

With virtually no warning, Cyclone Tracy struck Darwin. From late Christmas Eve through Christmas morning, the cyclone smashed through the city.

The Citizens

Many families had very little time to prepare. They quickly grabbed all of the safety equipment they could find. Hurrying into whatever safe room or area they could think of, they waited out the storm.

Kym Cluff of Darwin, Australia, was twelve years old when Cyclone Tracy came to town. Her mother did not survive the storm. "I remember looking at her, my mother. She only had one little cut on her leg. I kept thinking,

17

Dec. 20
Dec. 21
Bathurst Island
Dec. 22
Tropical Low
Tropical Cyclone
N
Arafura Sea
Dec. 23
Dec. 24
Darwin
AUSTRALIA
EUROPE
ASIA
AFRICA
INDIAN OCEAN
AUSTRALIA

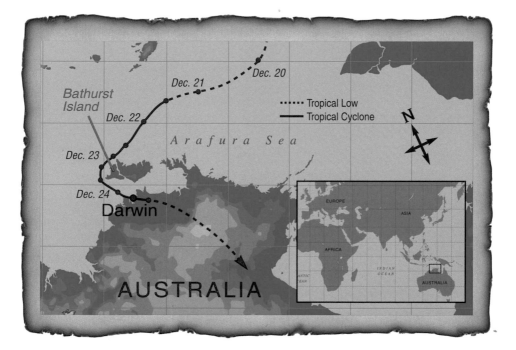

Cyclone Tracy made a sudden turn and aimed straight for Darwin, Australia.

there's nothing wrong with you. You're not hurt."[5] Cluff's mother, however, had suffered fatal internal injuries.

One victim lost his roof during the storm: "All you're surrounded by were brick walls. And nothing above you. Rain and wind sheeting in, and the noise, and sheets of iron flying. It was actually terrifying."[6]

The storm passed, leaving over 70 percent of Darwin destroyed. Homes, businesses, schools, and playgrounds were all gone. As one announcer described, "From the air, Darwin looks like a giant rubbish [garbage] dump."[7]

By Christmas morning, Darwin had lost all electric, water, communication, and sewage service.[8]

The Cleanup

In total, sixty-five people died in Darwin that night. Many others were injured. The city was in such devastation that evacuations were immediately ordered. Officials wanted to lower the population so that cleanup would be easier and less people would suffer from lack of services. The

Most of the town of Darwin was wiped out by the storm.

goal was to have over thirty thousand people leave the city. Most did. By December 31, 1974, there were only 10,638 people remaining in Darwin.[9]

However, many former residents commuted into Darwin to help cleanup. The country banded together to send support and aid to the suffering city. It was nearly a decade before the city was what its citizens would call "normal" once again. "There was a lot of anguish. . . . A lot of pain. No one knew how to deal with it. . . ," Kym Cluff explained.[10] The biggest hurdle of all for the citizens of Darwin would be to forget the memories of Cyclone Tracy's Christmas visit.

Many Darwin residents returned from Christmas vacation to find their homes wrecked by Cyclone Tracy.

CHAPTER

4

Andrew's Fury and Floyd's Floods

WITH ALL ITS COASTS EXPOSED TO HURRICANE tracks, the United States has seen many dangerous storms. The 1990s were no exception.

"The Wind Was Screaming"

On August 24, 1991, Hurricane Andrew slammed into Florida with sustained winds over 155 miles per hour. By August 26, 1991, the Category 5 storm was gone, leaving sixty-one deaths and over $20 billion in damages.

Ben Horenstein experienced Hurricane Andrew firsthand. "I will always remember the sound, you know how a trumpet squeals when the player is really straining? That was the sound at the front door. The wood was buckling and that seam between the double doors, the wind was screaming to get in."[1]

That sound arrived early that August morning. Many citizens had evacuated before the storm hit. Others stayed behind. They all hoped that the storm would not hit as hard as expected.

Unfortunately, the storm's strength left little unharmed. The violent wind and rain began well before Hurricane Andrew blew into southern Florida. In some areas, nearly a foot of rain fell in one day. As the eye wall made landfall, the damages worsened.

Although the fullest extent of the damage may never be known, it is estimated that seventy thousand homes were destroyed and fifty-six thousand other homes were significantly damaged.[2]

Huddled in the Darkness

Ben Horenstein was not alone during the storm. He survived along with his wife, Anne, their two sons, his sister, and her wheelchair-bound daughter. They all huddled together while the most severe part of the storm passed over his house. The power of the winds left an impression that Horenstein says will never be forgotten, "I was on my way to the back room to check out a noise when I saw the fence go, and I know how heavy that wood is!" As the wind continued to roar, large portions of the roof were blown away, leaving the house exposed to the storm.[3]

Horenstein also described the reaction of his neighbor,

Jack Lubin. ". . . We could hear a neighbor calling out, 'Benny? Anne?' So we . . . made our way outside," said Ben. "The neighbor was Jack, and he was crying. When he saw our house he was sure we were dead."[4]

Luiz Munoz also rode out the storm at home with his wife and three kids. The family of five crowded together in a hall closet using the ironing board to keep the door closed against the force of the winds. It was a traumatic experience for the whole family. Munoz said, "We will not be back here for a long, long time."[5] The Munozes

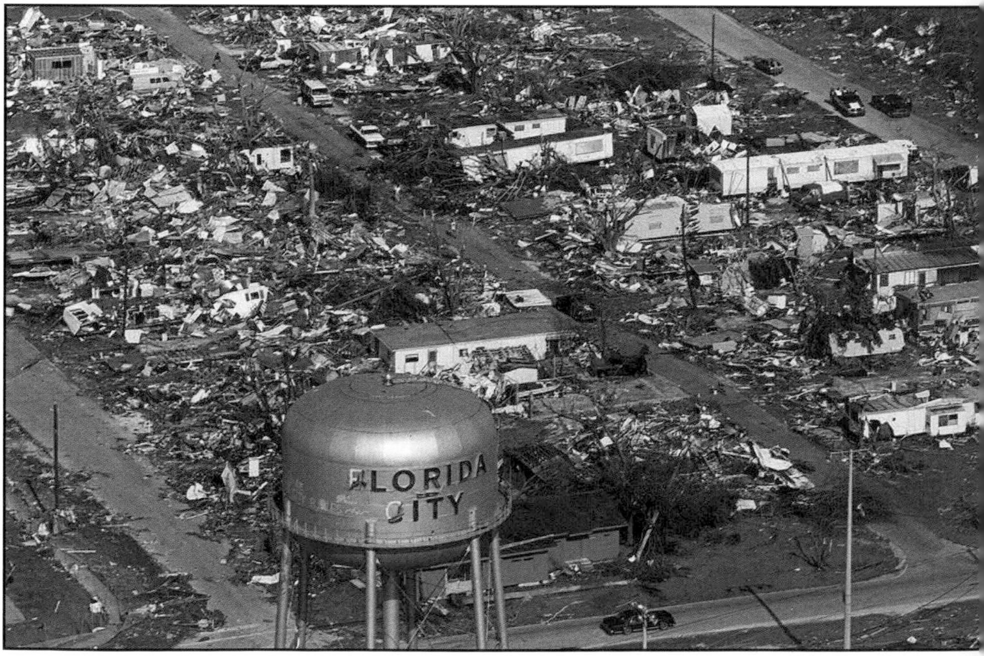
FLORIDA
CITY

Florida City was among the hardest hit by Hurricane Andrew. Most of its houses were completely flattened.

were not alone in that decision—many families chose to move somewhere else. As one local minister observed, "A lot of people were hurting, some people didn't even come back to get their stuff."[6]

Rebuilding for Years

The nation watched as the storm pounded the South Dade County area. As the clouds receded, help began to pour in. People of all backgrounds from all over the United States sent whatever support was necessary.

Within a day of the hurricane's departure, a disaster team from a Baptist church in Tennessee arrived. Over the next three months, they served seven hundred thousand meals to the victims of Hurricane Andrew. Thirteen other mobile soup kitchens came to the area courtesy of Baptist church members. More than forty quick-serve canteen trucks were sent by the Salvation Army. The National Guard and the Army Reserve ended up staying a full five years to help with the rebuilding process.[7]

The unity of the volunteers and the spirit of the victims amazed many. Jack Brown of Palm Beach County was one of those volunteers. "Others would come back talking about the damage. I came back talking about all the charity I saw."[8]

Students were also encouraged to help in the rebuilding. They were assigned tasks like cleanup and food donations.

Ted Allis sits in his wrecked home after Hurricane Andrew. A tree landed on the roof of his living room.

"I went from sitting at home to doing something," says Matt Goodman, who was twelve at the time. "It got my mind off my own problems and onto helping others."[9]

However, many remembered the storm with terror. Wind, even in small amounts, was very scary for some survivors. The United Methodist Committee on Relief brought in a science teacher from the Midwest to teach the kids to fly kites. Lynette Fields observes, "Many of

them had become frightened by wind, he taught them to love the wind again."[10]

A Monster Storm

At 6 A.M., September 17, 1999, a monster storm was born. Hurricane Floyd was six-hundred miles wide.[11] Winds sustained at 155, and peaked at 180 miles per hour, making it a category 4 hurricane.[12]

Official hurricane watches went into effect thirty-six hours before the storm was set to strike an area. Warnings came out within twenty-four hours. Over the next few days, these watches and warnings would be issued from Florida through Massachusetts.

Floyd first remained over 100 miles off the Florida coast. This was not much comfort, though. Its winds left 125,000 people without electric power. Bands of the storm also caused some of the worst flooding the state had seen in almost a decade.[13] Floyd barreled into the coast of North Carolina on September 16, 1999 with winds gusting to 100 miles per hour.

Landfall

In total, over 2 million people evacuated. It was the largest evacuation in United States history. Yet, still some remained behind. Calvin McGowan did not feel the evacuation was necessary. "I wouldn't stay for more than

135 mph winds," he said, "Most people's limit's about 100." His wife and son were with him. He said it sounded like "all the nails were coming out of the boards" of the house.[14] Authorities considered the family lucky to have survived.

Almost 480,000 homes and businesses lost electric power. Many people were without water, phones, and even shelter. It was an eventful night for many, but it was only the beginning of Floyd's wrath on the East Coast.

Rising Waters

In less than a day, fifteen inches of rain fell in North Carolina. Rivers began overflowing. The saturated ground

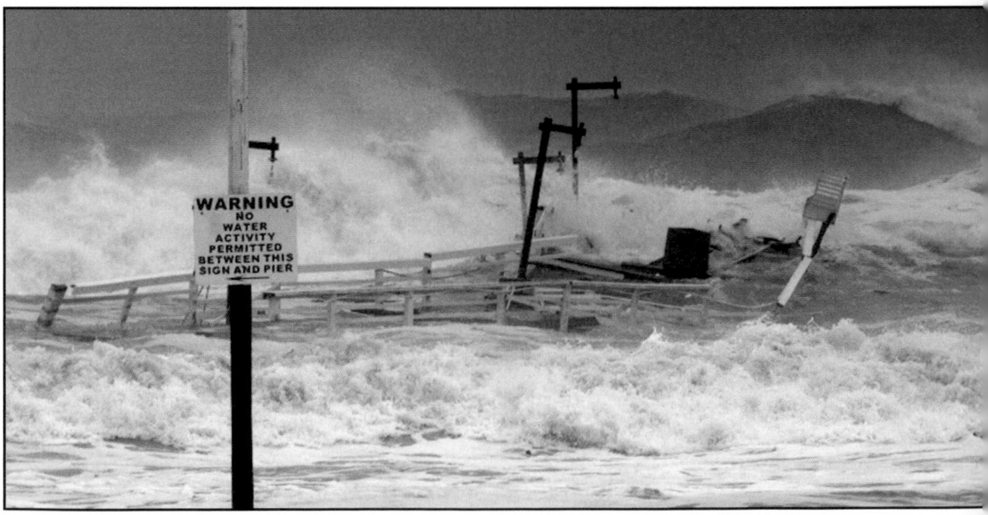
WARNING
NO
WATER
ACTIVITY
PERMITTED
BETWEEN THIS
SIGN AND PIER

When Hurricane Floyd came toward land, its storm surge collapsed this pier at Daytona Beach, Florida.

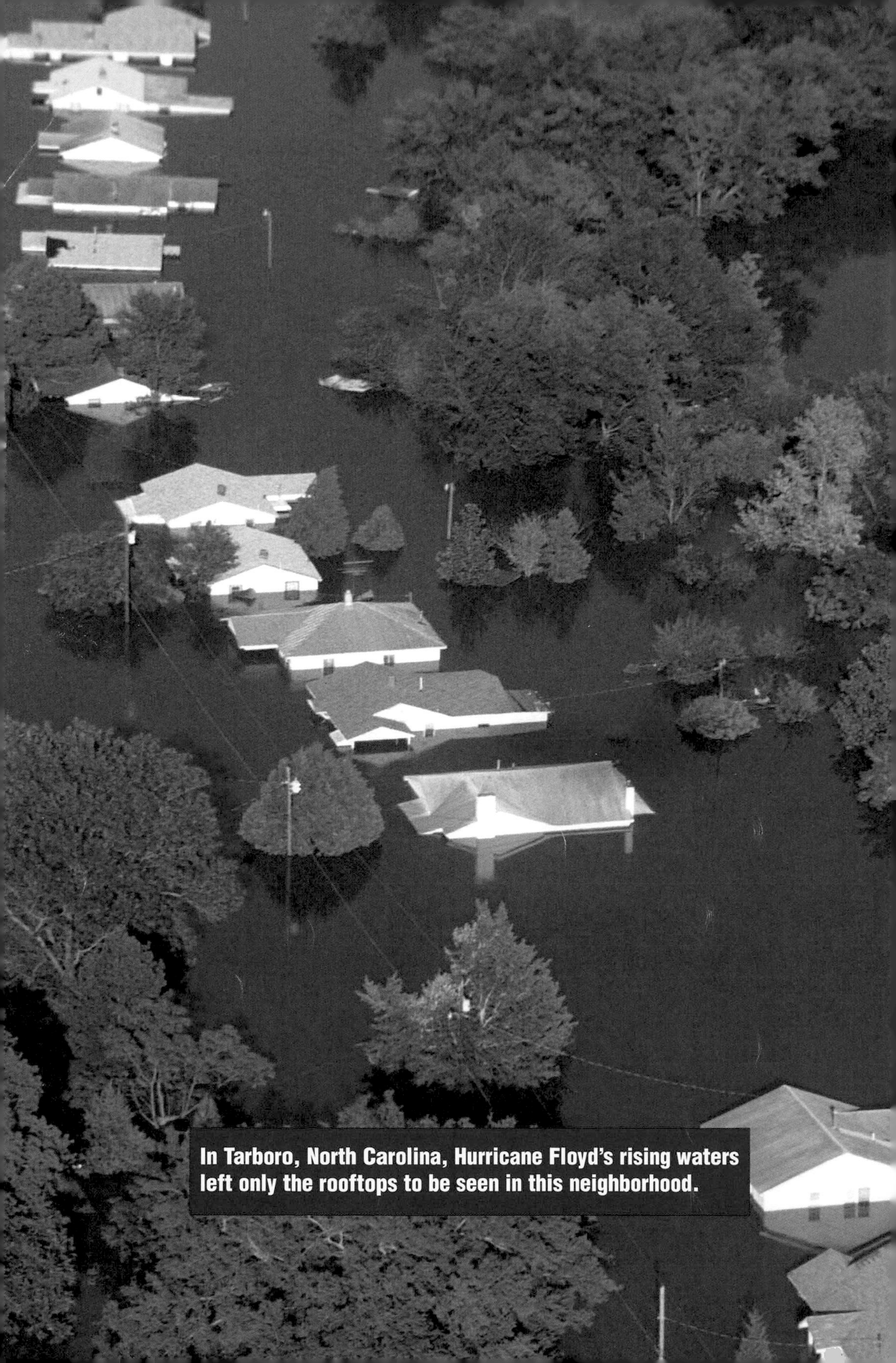

In Tarboro, North Carolina, Hurricane Floyd's rising waters left only the rooftops to be seen in this neighborhood.

could not take any more water. Rainfall filled streets.[15] Some homes were up to their rooftops in water. Over fifteen hundred flood survivors were rescued from rooftops and treetops.[16]

Greenville Marine, a North Carolina boat dealership, ended up completely underwater. ". . . now we have to start over," said owner Joe Vernelson. "I ain't a quitter, . . . But now the hard thing is getting motivated again."[17] An Oak Island resident agreed. "It looks like a war zone," said Joyce Odell. "It just makes you want to sit down and cry."[18]

Even after it was no longer a hurricane, Floyd continued to cause severe flooding all the way up the East Coast of the United States.

Rebuilding

In North Carolina, Vernelson and his family found hope in the community support. Volunteer help got them through the many days of recovery. "They came on a mission," recalls Vernelson. A group of young people spent the day cleaning and painting his boat dealership. "They restored my faith in the youth of America. It's funny how disasters either bring out the best or the worst in people. For most, it brought out the best."[19]

The Toll of Typhoon Tokage

O N OCTOBER 20, 2004, TYPHOON TOKAGE STRUCK western Japan with strong winds and massive waves. The fierce storm forced the evacuation of over eighteen thousand people, took the lives of ninety-two people, and injured over three hundred others.[1] At its peak, the storm stretched across a 500-mile radius.[2] A Meteorological Agency official stated that "such a huge typhoon is very rare."[3]

Tokage Hits Land

Miles Essex of Saga, Japan, survived the storm. "Some of the gusts of wind made the house vibrate and rattled the glasses in the cupboards, it felt as if the whole house was about to leave the ground," said Essex. "We were lucky,"

A giant wave crashes against a seawall in Japan during Typhoon Tokage.

he continued, "and escaped with merely a broken fence, a broken gutter and a roof tile missing."[4]

Others were not so fortunate. In total, 23,210 homes were severely damaged, while hundreds of others were completely destroyed. There were thousands of people who were forced to take refuge in temporary shelters.[5]

In Hyogo Prefecture, Japan, Stephanie Worrall remained trapped in her home for a full day. ". . . no electricity, phone, water or heat for almost 24 hours. The only road out was blocked by massive tree falls," Worrall said.

"As always, though, the community came together," she continued. "The farmers brought out their chainsaws and tools. Everyone worked to clear a path for the repair vehicles and finally at 6:30 P.M. we had power!"[6]

Okinawa Shuts Down

While Tokyo escaped major damages, many parts of Japan did not. Damage claims arising from Typhoon Tokage totaled 88.5 billion yen, which is equal to $839 million.[7]

Houses and roadways in Toyooka, Japan, were submerged in water due to flooding from Tokage.

A family is rescued from the top floor of their home

On the island of Okinawa, U.S. military bases prepared for the hit. At Kadena Air Base, 1st Lieutenant John Hurley of Kadena's 18th Weather Flight reported more than 4 inches of rain. In addition, the wind gusts ranged from 72 miles per hour to 89 miles per hour.[8]

While there were no reports of damage or injury on the base, the storm did manage to shut down everything in the area. It also injured civilians in cities near the base's location.[9]

All airports were closed, which stranded thirty-two thousand people. On Okinawa, at least eighty-four hundred people were left without power.[10]

Whether in Japan or any other area prone to tropical cyclones, a person should always be prepared during storm season.

33

6

Staying Safe

TROPICAL CYCLONES ARE A POWERFUL FORCE. IT CAN be frightening to hear that one is approaching. However, if you prepare and stay informed, you have a good chance of being uninjured. Be prepared for watches and warnings. Follow the advice of the experts. Always decide in advance how you will respond.

Forecasting

In order to send out accurate forecasts, the weather centers must study the storms very carefully. Satellite systems monitor sea surface temperature, atmospheric pressure, and the storm's track through advanced computer systems. In addition, "hurricane hunters" fly planes into the eye of the storm in order to get the most exact information possible.[1] While satellite and radar

systems can give the forecasters a good basis to predict a hurricane's path, the hurricane hunters can bring back data that makes the forecasts up to 30 percent more accurate. During each mission, the hunters fly through the eye of the storm many times. They can pinpoint exactly where the center of the storm is located. They can also determine if the storm is strengthening or weakening and transmit the exact wind speed and direction.[2]

All of this data is combined and used to build models that predict the most likely path of a storm.

A hurricane hunter flies directly over the eye of a hurricane.

35

Forecasting is very important because it gives people the warning time they need to safely prepare them and their loved ones for a coming storm.

Watches and Warnings

Hurricanes take several days to develop. When a hurricane is within thirty-six hours of a area, a hurricane watch is issued. If a hurricane watch is issued, residents must begin to prepare for the worst.[3]

A hurricane warning is issued next. A warning means that hurricane-force winds could arrive within twenty-four hours. Residents must react immediately. Some storms are tricky, like Cyclone Tracy. They can move fast, and even change direction. If a warning is issued, follow all instructions from authorities.[4]

If an evacuation is ordered, officials feel the area will be too dangerous for residents. You should always leave the area when an evacuation is ordered. You may want to protect your house from a hurricane, but it is better to protect yourself by getting somewhere safe.

Preparations

Every family should have a disaster plan. This plan gives everyone a guideline and a job. It means that instead of panicking or being unprepared, people will work together to ensure their safety. Here are some ways to get ready for a storm.

If You Live in a Hurricane-Prone Area

- Find out if you are in an "evacuation zone."
- Place all important documents in waterproof containers or safe-deposit boxes.
- Keep a list and photographs of valuables for insurance purposes.
- Keep all trees trimmed away from the house.
- Put together an emergency kit—batteries, flashlights, radio, blankets, first-aid kit, a 3-day supply of food and water, extra clothing, emergency tools, and any special items needed for infants, the elderly, or disabled.

When a Storm Watch Is Issued

- Fill prescriptions; drugstores may be closed or damaged for weeks.
- Fill vehicles with gas, in case of evacuations.
- Take out cash for necessities.
- Fill sinks/bathtubs with spare water, in case your house loses its water service.
- Move all easily blown objects inside.

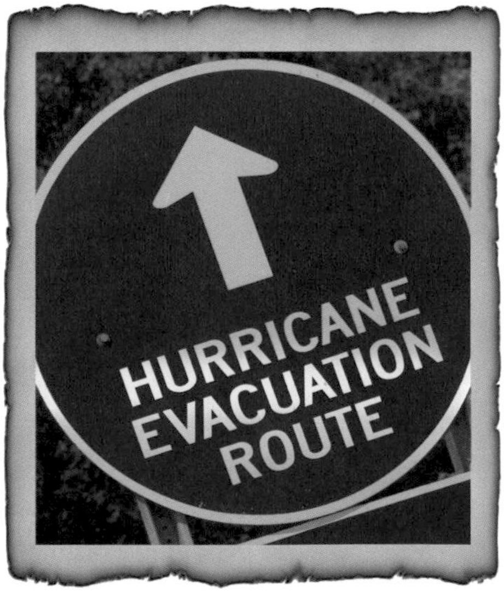
HURRICANE
EVACUATION
ROUTE

It is important for a family to have more than one evacuation plan. That way, if a road is impassable, there is another way to escape.

When a Storm Warning is Issued

- Check T.V. or radio for announcements.
- Even if not ordered to evacuate, you may want to go somewhere that is out of the storm's projected path. If you cannot, stay inside, away from windows.
- If the storm passes directly over, there will be a period of calm before the winds start up again. Stay in a safe place.
- Evacuate if ordered to do so. Avoid flooded roads when evacuating.
- Be aware that a hurricane can spawn tornadoes even after it passes.[5]

Be sure to add your family's specific needs to the list and help your parents when the time comes.

Helping Out

Only a small portion of the world is directly affected by tropical cyclones. Yet everyone can help. After a hurricane, residents need shelter, food, and clothing.

Many programs exist to help people in their time of need. The American Red Cross, along with the Federal Emergency Management Agency, get involved. Also, many community groups and churches join the efforts.

Most people cannot help directly at the site of the damage. However, schools can hold fund-raisers, clothing drives, or collect food to send to affected families. People

A relief worker in Fort Lauderdale, Florida, hands out a box of bottled water in the wake of Hurricane Frances in 2004.

can also donate money. It is best to do so through a recognized organization, such as the Red Cross. That way the money will go to those most in need.

Tropical cyclones in any form can create tragedy. Yet everyone can help to bring hope and safety back to a hurting community.

Deadliest Hurricanes, Typhoons, and Cyclones

World's Deadliest Hurricanes, Typhoons, and Cyclones			
Date	Location	Description	Number Killed
November 12–13, 1970	East Pakistan	Cyclone and tidal waves	200,000*
April 30, 1991	Southeast Bangladesh	Cyclone leaves 9 million homeless	131,000
October 5, 1864	Calcutta, India	Cyclone	70,000
October 16, 1942	Bengal India	Cyclone	40,000
June 1–2, 1965	East Pakistan	Cyclone	30,000
May 28–29, 1963	East Pakistan	Cyclone	22,000
November 19, 1977	Andhra Pradesh, India	Cyclone and tidal wave	20,000
May 11–12, 1965	East Pakistan	Cyclone	17,000
October 26– November 4, 1998	Honduras, Nicaragua, and Guatemala	Hurricane Mitch	11,000
September 18, 1906	Hong Kong	Typhoon and tidal wave	10,000

*100,000 more went missing

Source: "Major Storms," *Infoplease.com*, © 2005, <http://www.infoplease.com/ipa/A0001441.html> (March 4, 2005).

Deadliest Hurricanes in the United States		
Date	Location	Number Killed
September 8, 1900	Galveston, Texas	6,000–8,000
September 6–20, 1928	Southeast Florida	1,836
August 28, 1893	Georgia and South Carolina	1,000
September 2–15, 1919	Florida Keys, Louisiana, and Southern Texas	600
September 10–22, 1938	Long Island, New York, and southern New England	600

Source: "U.S. Hurricanes," *Infoplease.com*, ©2005, <http://www.infoplease.com/ipa/A0001443.html> (March 4, 2005).

Chapter Notes

Chapter 1. A Record-Breaking Season

1. Abby Goodnough, "Another Hurricane Roars Across Mid-Florida," *The New York Times*, September 27, 2004, p. 22.

2. John L. Beven, II, "Tropical Cyclone Report: Hurricane Frances," *National Hurricane Center: Tropical Prediction Center*, December 17, 2004, <http://www.nhc.noaa.gov/2004frances.shtml?> (March 4, 2005).

3. Ibid.

4. Stacy R. Stewart, "Tropical Cyclone Report: Hurricane Ivan," *National Hurricane Center: Tropical Prediction Center*, December 16, 2004, <http://www.nhc.noaa.gov/2004ivan.shmtl?> (March 4, 2005).

5. Goodnough, p. 22.

6. Miles B. Lawrence and Hugh D. Cobb, "Tropical Cyclone Report: Hurricane Jeanne," *National Hurricane Center: Tropical Prediction Center*, November 22, 2004, <http://www.nhc.noaa.gov/2004jeanne.shmtl?> (March 4, 2005).

7. Melanie Payne, "Terror lives when safety comes crashing down," *The News-Press Fort Meyers*, December 5, 2004, p. A8.

8. Lawrence and Cobb.

9. James C. McKinley, "Weary, Angry Haitians Dig Out of Storm," *The New York Times*, September 24, 2004, p. 3.

10. Ibid.

Chapter 2. The Science of Hurricanes, Typhoons, and Cyclones

1. Bob Sheets and Jack Williams, *Hurricane Watch: Forecasting the Deadliest Storms on Earth* (New York: Vintage Books, 2001), pp. 285–286.

2. Ibid.

3. Reader's Digest, *Weather* (New York: Reader's Digest Association Inc., 1997), pp. 96–102.

4. Ibid.

5. Ibid.

6. American Red Cross, *Hurricanes . . . Unleashing Nature's*

41

Fury, U.S. Department of Commerce: National Oceanic and Atmospheric Administration, August 2001, p. 4.

7. Michael Allaby, *Hurricanes* (New York: Facts on File Inc., 1997), p. 51.

8. Jeffrey Rosenfeld, *Eye of the Storm: Inside the World's Deadliest Hurricanes, Tornadoes, and Blizzards* (New York: Plenum Trade, 1999), pp. 73, 113.

9. Ibid.

10. "Worldwide Tropical Cyclone Names," *National Hurricane Center*, n.d., <http://www.nhc.noaa.gov/aboutnames.shtml> (January 30, 2005).

11. "How are Hurricanes Named?" *For Kids Only—Earth Science Enterprise*, n.d., <http://kids.earth.nasa.gov/archive/hurricane/names.html> (February 25, 2005).

12. "The Saffir-Simpson Hurricane Scale," *National Hurricane Center*, September 19, 2003, <http://www.nhc.noaa.gov/aboutsshs.shtml> (February 25, 2005).

Chapter 3. A Tragic Christmas Day

1. "Darwin and the Northern Territory in 1974," *Cyclone Tracy*, n.d, <http://www.ntlib.nt.gov.au/tracy/advanced/1974.htm> (January 30, 2005).

2. "Fact Sheet 176," *Cyclone Tracy*, n.d., <http://www.naa.gov.au/fsheets/FS176.htm> (January 30, 2005).

3. Ibid.

4. Ibid.

5. "AM Archive—Cyclone Tracy—25 Years on," *AM Archive*, December 24, 1999, <http://www.abc.net.au/am/stories/s75342.htm> (July 21, 2004).

6. Ibid.

7. Ibid.

8. Ibid.

9. "Response to Cyclone Tracy—Evacuation," *Cyclone Tracy*, n.d., <http://www.ntlib.nt.gov.au/tracy/basic/evaluation.html> (February 25, 2005).

10. "Fact Sheet 176."

Chapter 4. Andrew's Fury and Floyd's Floods

1. Jonathan King, "The Screaming Winds Trumpeted Disaster," *Sun-Sentinel.com*, August 18, 2002, <http://pqasb.pqarchiver. com/sun_sentinel/151975681.html?did=151975681&FMT=ABS&FMTS= FT&date=Aug+18%2C+2002&author=JONATHON+KING++STAFF+ WRITER&desc=THE+SCREAMING+WINDS+TRUMPETED+ DISASTER> (February 28, 2005).

2. Ibid.

3. Ibid.

4. Ibid.

5. Ibid.

6. "Dade Residents Stunned as Storm Shatters Lives," *Sun-Sentinel.com*, August 25, 1992, <http://pqasb.pqarchiver.com/ sun_sentinel/89685731.html?did=89685731&FMT=ABS&FMTS=FT& date=Aug+25%2C+1992&author=Staff+reports&desc=DADE+ RESIDENTS+STUNNED+AS+STORM+SHATTERS+LIVES> (February 28, 2005).

7. Deborah Sharp, "Floridians Recall Andrew's Rage," *USA Today*, August 23, 2002, p. A03.

8. Ibid.

9. James D. Davis, "Answered Prayers; Within Hours of Andrew's Departure, Religious Groups Joined Forces to Provide Victims with a Place to Call Home," *Sun-Sentinel.com*, August 24, 2002, <http://pqasb.pqarchiver.com/sun_sentinel/155120001. html?did=155120001&FMT=ABS&FMTS=FT&date=Aug+24%2C+ 2002&author=James+D.+Davis++Religion+Editor&desc=ANSWERED+ PRAYERS+%3B+WITHIN+HOURS+OF+ANDREW%27S+ DEPARTURE%2C+RELIGIOUS+GROUPS+JOINED+FORCES+TO+ PROVIDE+VICTIMS+WITH+A+PLACE+TO+CALL+HOME> (February 28, 2005).

10. Ibid.

11. "Hurricane Floyd Reports," *The Disaster Center*, n.d., <http://www.disastercenter.com/hurricf9.htm> (January 30, 2005).

12. Ibid.

13. "Floyd is Not Done Yet," *Detroit Free Press*, September 17,

1999, <http://www.freep.com/news/nw/qfloyd17.htm> (January 30, 2005).

14. Ibid.

15. "Floyd's Floods Strand Residents," *USA Today*, September 20, 1999, <http://www.usatoday.com/weather/hurricane/1999> (July 22, 2004).

16. Ibid.

17. "Greenville Marine Survives Hurricane," *Greenville Marine & Sport Center, Inc.*, n.d., <http://www.greenvillemarine.com/hurricanestory.htm> (July 22, 2004).

18. Ibid.

19. Ibid.

Chapter 5. The Toll of Typhoon Tokage

1. "Deadly Typhoon tears across Japan," *BBC News*, October 21, 2004, <http://news.bbc.co.uk/1/hi/world/asia-pacific/3759624.stm> (January 30, 2005).

2. Ibid.

3. Ibid.

4. Ibid.

5. "Death toll rises to 77 in Japan typhoon," *CTV*, October 22, 2004, <http://www.ctv.ca/servlet/ArticleNews/story/CTVNews/1098441539576_16?hub=World> (January 3, 2005).

6. "Typhoon Tokage's death toll reaches 80," *The Japan Times Online*, n.d., <http://www.japantimes.co.jp/cgi-bin/getarticle.p15?nn20041024a4.htm> (January 3, 2005).

7. "Typhoon Tokage insurance claims are estimated at 88.5 Bln Yen," *Bloomberg.com*, November 17, 2004, <http://www.bloomberg.com/apps/news?pid=10000101&sid=aU7Qh2YpFgIA&refer=japan> (January 30, 2005).

8. Dave Ornaver, "Typhoon Tokage pelts Okinawa, moves towards Japan," *Stars and Stripes*, October 21, 2004, <http://www.estripes.com/article.asp?section=104&article=24164&archive=true> (January 30, 2005).

9. Ibid.

10. Ibid.

Chapter 6. Staying Safe

1. "Chasing the Storm," *Windows to the Universe*, n.d., <http://www.windows.ucar.edu/tour/link=/earth/Atmosphere/hurricane/hunters.html&edu=high> (January 30, 2005).

2. Ibid.

3. "Hurricanes: Weather Watches, Warnings, and Forecasts," *National Oceanic and Atmospheric Administration*, n.d., <http://hurricanes.noaa.gov> (January 30, 2005).

4. Ibid.

5. "Are You Ready For A Hurricane?" *American Red Cross*, July 1998, <http://www.redcross.org/static/file_cont207_lang0_94cont207_lang0_94.pdf> (March 4, 2005).

Glossary

American Red Cross—An independent nonprofit agency that deals with national and international disasters by supplying support, funds, and other assistance to suffering populations.

Coriolis effect—The deflection of winds and ocean currents from their original direction due to the earth's rotation, causing them to then circulate around high- and low-pressure systems.

eye—The center of a tropical cyclone, the eye has no wind.

eye wall—The stormiest area of a tropical cyclone that rotates around the eye.

Federal Emergency Management Agency (FEMA)—The federally funded agency that handles all aspects of emergency management, including planning, funding support, supplying necessary services, and determining the level of support a specific emergency will receive.

hurricane season—The time in the United States when hurricane activity is most likely to occur—June 1 through November 30.

meteorologist—A professional who deals with weather science, such as short- or long-term prediction of conditions.

outer bands—Stormy areas that stretch out from the eye wall.

Saffir-Simpson Scale—The universal scale used to rank the level of damage a tropical cyclone causes.

tropical cyclone—A violent storm originating over tropical or subtropical waters, characterized by violent rainstorms and high-velocity cyclonic winds; a hurricane, typhoon, or cyclone.

Further Reading

Books

Challen, Paul. *Hurricanes and Typhoon Alert!* New York: Crabtree Publications, 2004.

Davis, Pete. *The Hurricane: Face to Face with Nature's Deadliest Storms.* New York: Henry Holt and Company, LLC, 2000.

Longshore, David. *Encyclopedia of Hurricanes, Typhoons, and Cyclones.* New York: Checkmark Books, 2000.

Seymour, Simon. *Hurricanes.* New York: HarperCollins, 2003.

Williams, Jack, and Bob Sheets. *Hurricane Watch: Forecasting the Deadliest Storms on Earth.* New York: Vintage, 2001.

Internet Addresses

The Hurricane Hunters
<http://www.hurricanehunters.com>

National Oceanic and Atmospheric Administration: Hurricanes
<http://hurricanes.noaa.gov>

Hurricane Preparedness
<http://www.nhc.noaa.gov>
On the left, under the "Hurricane Awareness" heading, click on "Be Prepared." On the left, click on "Basics."

Index